This book would not have been possible without the love, support, and encouragement of my daughter, Beeta.

# Unbridled

Just before seven on a rainy Sunday morning in March 1988, an Amtrak train pulled into Penn station. Aboard the slowing locomotive, Nora Wheeler, dressed in worn white sneakers, a black sweatshirt and faded jeans, peered through her rain-specked window. It had been a long, boring ride. All along the way, Nora had reflected on her life, torn between flashes of rage, self-pity and hopes for a brighter future.

Nora was a long haul from Crestline, California where she'd spent the last several years residing in a small mountain cabin with her mother and two younger brothers. Nora—a tall, slim, twenty-two-year-old woman with hazel-brown, almond-shaped eyes and dark brown hair—was returning to her childhood home in search of work, security and perhaps even peace. The long train ride, which she thought she'd enjoy, had bored her. Throughout its length, she'd rehashed her life, wishing she'd flown.

As the train eased to a stop, Nora rose from her seat. Pulling a small black suitcase and tattered purple backpack from the overhead rack, she smiled at the young African-American woman who seemed so overwhelmed by three small children and all their bags. Nora walked off the train, past the passenger's information desk and toward the street. Back in New York after ten years, she'd be living in Brooklyn with her Aunt Lil and Uncle Gerry Whitcomb for the time being. Hopefully not for long, though, one of her top priorities was to get out on her own.

Since graduating from a San Bernardino beautician's school three years prior, Nora had worked in her sleepy, California mountain town. When the shop's owner closed her business six months before, Nora sought another job. Finding nothing "on the hill", she called her Aunt Lil, who owned a New York salon, to see if employment was even remotely possible. To Nora's surprise, it was. Her mother resisted initially, but eventually relented.

Nora was eager to get to be done with traveling. She found the subway entrance then descended into the vaguely familiar subterranean bustle. Forty minutes and eighteen stops later, she arrived in Brooklyn. It was raining when she emerged from underground. 'Damn rain,' she thought. 'That's the last thing I need.' She considered phoning her Uncle Gerry to ask for a ride, but she'd been sitting for so long that she decided that walking would do her good. Besides, she'd envisioned getting there on her own. After extracting and opening her umbrella, she trudged up the street.

She walked a couple blocks to First Street then headed north on Third. Waiting for a light to change, she hugged her light suitcase against her body. When the light turned green, she leapt over a puddle then scurried on. It seemed to take forever, but at last she reached her relations' familiar brownstone row house. From beneath her umbrella, she gazed up at the tall, slim building. Fond memories of family gatherings washed over her.

She started up the short concrete path that bisected a tiny front lawn, then ascended four steps. After setting her suitcase on the stoop she closed her umbrella. Standing on the porch she remembered listening to her Aunt Lil's stories before going to bed. After a deep breath, she rang the doorbell. Her dapper uncle opened the door.

"Hello, Uncle Gerry," Nora said.

"Ah, hello honey," he replied, pressing open the screen. "You came all this way in the rain! I can't believe you wouldn't tell us your arrival time."

"It would've spoiled my surprise," Nora beamed.

Stepping out, he hugged her. "It's so nice to see you, dear!"

Hugging him back, she asked, "You too, Uncle Gerry. You *are* surprised, right?"

"More delighted," he said releasing her, "but sure, surprised too."

"Good!" Nora exclaimed.

Taking her suitcase in one of his hands and her shoulder with the other, he ushered her in. "My God, Nora, you've grown up since I last saw you! You're a woman!"

"You haven't changed a bit, Uncle Gerry."

A little smile played his lips and an amused twinkle lit his eyes. "Well, we've all changed some," Gerry responded, "some of us just more noticeably." Gerry set Nora's suitcase down in the tinny foyer. The same large, beautiful landscape oil painting she remembered decorated the wall. "How was your trip, sweetheart?"

Shifting from the painting the wider setting, Nora answered, "Boring! The last hours on that train seemed like an eternity! I thought I'd love seeing the country, but all I did was obsess on old wounds."

"Well, you're here now. Welcome! How are your mother and brothers?"

The question made Nora slightly sad. "I'd like to say good, but complicated would be more accurate."

"Well, we don't have to delve into that now."

"Thank you, Uncle Gerry."

"You're welcome."

Her kind, thoughtful and intelligent uncle was one of the happiest, most contented people she'd ever known. A tall, lankly man in late middle age, he had a kind face and wore thick glasses over mischievous blue eyes. His wide suspenders and snappy plaid trousers perfectly suited his tousled silver hair. A librarian for many years, his life revolved around reading and other simple pleasures. A great wit, Gerry put people at ease under almost any circumstances. The house was, as always, neat and beautifully decorated. The warm interior smelled of coffee.

"Where's Auntie Lil?" Nora asked.

"At work," Gerry answered.

"But it's Sunday. Is she at her salon?"

"No, a funeral home."

"Oh," Nora said. Any mention of Lil's second job always made Nora uneasy. Lil, the owner of *My Escape Nail & Hair Salon*, also did make up for several funeral homes; desairology, it was called. Although Nora was a beautician also, the darker side Aunt Lil's work baffled and even somewhat appalled her.

Smiling at Nora's expression Gerry said, "She'll be home soon. All covered in blood no doubt."

Nora couldn't laugh. Dodging Gerry's jibe, she changed the subject, "I can't wait to see her. I've missed you guys so much."

"We've missed you too, hon. We're so glad you've come to stay with us."

Gerry escorted Nora into the living room. Everything was in perfect keeping with the souls that lived there. Nothing was extremely expensive or ostentatiously extravagant, but everything was exquisitely placed. A welcoming fire was blazing upon the hearth. The sofa looked new but Lil and Gerry's same old worn recliners were still there. As they sat on the couch, Gerry said, "Lil was called to do makeup on one of her long-term salon customers. It's not one of her regular desairology venues. They usually handle restorative cosmetology themselves, but the woman requested Lil."

"Oh," Nora responded, still uncomfortable with the topic.

"Are you hungry, Nora?"

Despite thinking the segue from death to food odd, Nora responded, "Famished. I was so rushed to get here that I didn't eat."

"I'll make us some breakfast," Gerry offered. Rising, he continued, "Why don't you freshen up and then join me in the kitchen?"

"Thanks, Uncle Gerry." Nora rose then gave Gerry another hug and a kiss. "I won't be long."

She went to the first floor bathroom. After a few minutes, she entered the kitchen. "Do you have any aspirin, Uncle Gerry? That train ride gave me a headache."

"Why don't you eat something first?" Gerry suggested. "I'll get you some aspirin after breakfast."

Nora sat down at the kitchen table. After filling both their cups with coffee, Gerry went back to his cooking. Before long, he was setting down a feast: scrambled eggs, bacon, bread, butter and homemade strawberry jam. To Nora, the meal had significance beyond mere hospitality; she felt she'd found both love and support. When they'd eaten and cleared their plates, she said, "Thanks for breakfast, Uncle Gerry. I really enjoyed it."

"You're very welcome, honey."

They returned to the living room. Nora sank into the couch as Gerry opted for his recliner. He lit a cigarette and they chatted. Nora gave a short account of her long days on the train and then told of losing her job. She spoke of how unhappy her mother had been when Nora decided to leave. Somehow, Gerry's compassionate, quiet listening opened her emotional floodgates.

Nora talked nonstop, telling far more than she'd intended to of how she'd been feeling since her father's suicide some years prior. She spoke of how she had absolutely no friends her own age and of how much her mother had withered since her husband's death; how stressful living with her had become, especially after Nora lost her job. They'd been fighting over so many little things that Nora decided, despite her mother's protests, to leave.

"Mom and I needed some distance and time to sort things out," she said. "We never reached any sort of resolution. I didn't know what I was doing there anymore. I just felt like I had to escape, that I needed to put that whole world behind me. All that California means to me is Father's failure and death. It hurts so much. I can't believe Mother stays there. She seems to have no aspirations anymore. I never thought I'd mind her pressuring me to work as a maid, but I did. I still do. I think it's because… I don't think she'll ever move on. I think she'll die that way. For some reason, I began feeling that that's what she wanted for me too: A bitter life made worse by a bitter job."

She talked and talked. The more she spoke, the more downcast she became. Finally, she choked on her words and began crying. Holding her face in her hands, she wailed, "I'm so confused, Uncle Gerry! I don't know what to do with my life!" She wiped her face on her sleeve.

Of course, Gerry knew the back-story: Nora's dad's suicide was, most believed, due to the loss of his once extensive holdings in a Ponzi scheme some thirteen years before. He hadn't killed himself until years after the great loss, but the fuse to his demise had burnt inexorably. His half-hearted efforts to find a new life in California hadn't, as the family had hoped, doused it. "I'm so sorry, honey," Gerry said. "I didn't mean to bring all this up again. You're obviously tired. I'm sorry."

"It's not your fault, Uncle Gerry," Nora sobbed. "I can't believe I'm rehashing all this garbage again. I just never seem to get over it. My childhood here was all happiness and light and California was pure misery."

Uncomfortably, Gerry lit another cigarette. Staring sympathetically across the coffee table, he leaned forward. "You're still wounded, honey. It's a heavy load you've been carrying. It's good you're here. You need time. Time heals everything. Even so, you've got to move on with your life now. When nearly all the power of your mind is moving in a certain direction, it's not easy to turn away from it, but you have to."

"I know, Uncle Gerry," she said, nervously toying with a pinkie ring, "but I still feel such *hatred* for that damn Dennis Pino. His schemes caused us so much misery! He ruined so many families! Every night, I wish him all the pain in the world and pray he dies horribly! I mean it! I actually *pray* for that! I've tried to let go of it, but I *can't*."

Gerry rose then came to Nora. Sitting beside her, he put his arm around her. Looking into her eyes, he said, "This is life, honey." Rubbing her back, he went on, "You have to understand, God didn't put us here for pure fun. Suffering and torment are parts of life. You just need to let go of these memories. Lil and I will help; we'll take care of you. Right now you need a proper rest. How about, go upstairs and relax. If you still want to talk about this later, we will."

Nora's cheeks were wet with tears. Doubting she'd ever want to talk about it again but knowing she would, she hugged Gerry and sobbed, "Thank you Uncle Gerry, thank you so much."

Filled with the home's love and warmth, she felt a little less of the complex bitterness she'd tasted since leaving Brooklyn so many years ago. Still, she was exhausted. Her head still ached and now she was feeling slightly ill. Trying to regain some composure, she wiped her tears. "Now that I'm here, I think I'll have more energy to focus. I'd like to study, to get a good job. I never stopped writing. I'd like to write and think. Above all, I'd like to own myself."

"That sounds great," Gerry said, "but for now you need to rest." He stood. "We'll get you past those tears. I see your pain but it's time to move on. We'll help."

More comforted than put-off by good-hearted clichés, Nora nodded.

Pausing, Gerry asked, "Would you like more coffee?"

Smiling, Nora said, "I thought you wanted me to rest."

"Hah. Sure I do. No offense, darling, but the way you're looking it'd take more than a few cups of coffee to keep you awake."

"Thanks, Uncle," Nora said, Still the flatterer, I see.

"As always."

"You're right though. Coffee won't keep me up. And two aspirins?"

"Oh yes, I forgot the aspirin. Sorry." He sort of bounced into the kitchen. His upbeat disposition never ceased to amaze Nora. Shortly, he returned carrying a painted tray loaded with refilled coffee cups, cream, a glass of water and Tylenol.

"I couldn't find any aspirin. I hope Tylenol's OK."

"Of course."

He placed the tray on the coffee table. Settling back into his recliner chair, he took up his coffee. They didn't say anything for some minutes. Nora couldn't help smiling at how comfortable it was. In some ways, she felt she'd never left. The interceding years felt somehow unreal. Eventually, Gerry offered from out of the blue, "You've got a lot working in your life, honey."

Nearly laughing, Nora asked, "Where'd that come from, Uncle?"

He shrugged. "From my thoughts. You have a trade and a sharp mind, honey. I can't tell you how happy I am to hear you say you're still writing. And, if you don't mind my saying so, you're quite beautiful."

"What if I do mind?"

"Then you're not. Regardless, focus more on opportunities than anchors, dear. Leave behind things that diminish you."

"Thanks, Uncle Gerry. You're sweet."

"Right now, you look exhausted. Would you like to go upstairs and rest? Lil's got your room ready."

"I don't want to sleep," Nora answered, "I'd rather talk."

"I know, honey, but... Did you sleep on that train at all?"

"Barely. It was more like occasional blackouts."

"Long trips take their toll. Why not get some rest? I'll have Lil wake you when she comes in."

Nodding wearily, Nora said, "OK." Rising along with Gerry, she said, "Thanks again for having me. And for breakfast." With that she gave him yet another hug and kiss. They walked to the staircase. Before going up, Nora said, "Sorry if I soured your day, Uncle Gerry."

"Don't think that, honey. You didn't. I'm so happy to see you that it almost hurts. And I'm glad you're still comfortable enough to talk to me."

Clutching her suitcase and backpack, Nora climbed the narrow staircase. She soon entered the small, familiar room. Meticulously clean, its walls were covered with soft white and pink wallpaper, yellowed with age. Framed pictures of her dead grandparents and other family members adorned the walls, dresser, desk and nightstands. 'They surround me like angels,' she thought.

She set her suitcase in an armchair. She opened it and pulled out a family photo of her own, the only one she possessed. The image within the tarnished frame—depicting her father, mother, two

14

younger brothers and herself—was taken in Riverside, a year after their move to California. The palm trees, smiles and blue skies belied their life. She walked to a nightstand and placed the photo alongside another and an old Bible.

She unpacked her clothes and laid them inside an ancient dark wood armoire. After undressing, she turned down the soft pink comforter. Sitting upon the bed, she plucked her photo back off the nightstand. Her eyes were watering again. She gave it a kiss and then hugged it. She put the photo back then lied down and drew up the blankets. The old brass bed was unbelievably comfortable. It was nearly noon and fully light out. Sunlight poured through lace curtains as she drifted off to sleep.

Desairology?

Aunt Nora's soft voice was cutting through the grey-black,
"Nora, honey, wake up." Drowsily, Nora shifted beneath her aunt's
gentle shaking. "Nora, love, hello. Wake up."

Slowly, Nora opened her eyes. Lil was sitting on the bed,
smiling down at her. Drinking in the woman's warm, dark eyes,
Nora's face lit up. Lil was made up with light pink lipstick, rouge
and eyeliner. She was wearing, as always, that little rope of pearls.
Her dark brown hair was perfect. She looked as if she'd just come
from her beauty parlor. To Nora she looked divinely fashioned,
beautiful in every sense of the word, possessed of a remarkable
degree of soul, strength and kindness.

Smiling, Nora sat up. She hugged Lil and kissed her. Nora's
eyes filled with tears again. Oh, she'd missed her aunt so much. She
didn't want to let her go, not ever. But she did. Leaning away, she

again absorbed the sight of her beautiful, kind aunt, who looked so elegant in her black cashmere sweater and dark skirt.

"How are you, my love?" Lil asked, smilingly touching Nora's hair.

"Great!" Nora replied, taking her aunt's free hand, "just a little tired."

Lil leaned in. After kissing Nora's forehead, she said, "I am so happy you're here, honey."

"Me too, Auntie Lil. Thank you so much for talking my mom into it."

"Oh honey, it was my pleasure." Standing, Lil said, "Take a shower if you'd like but come down soon. We have so much to talk about."

Stretching, Nora asked, "What time is it?"

Lil checked her watch. "Twenty till six."

"Wow, I never sleep in the afternoon. I don't usually nap well."

"I guess you needed it, honey." Leaning down to pet her niece once more, Lil went on, "Dinner will be ready soon. Gerry's got something special for you."

"Thank you, Auntie. I'll be down in a few minutes."

Nora loved all of her three aunts, but Lil's generosity, patience, artistic abilities with makeup and the fact that she was always there for her made Nora's bond with Aunt Lil seem almost unworldly. Nora got out of bed and went to the shower. Closing her eyes beneath the streaming water, she remembered how, only twelve years before, everything had seemed so secure.

After drying off, Nora pulled on a clean t-shirt and sweat pants. As she went downstairs, the aroma of roast beef wafted up to greet her. Standing in the kitchen entry unnoticed by her relations, Nora felt she was in the presence of two superior souls. Gerry's atmosphere gave peace and comfort to everybody around him. Lil seemed more grounded, but her human elements were so wonderfully blended that she was invariably singled out as a person in bloom. Just being near them made everything better.

Gerry spotted her. "What are you doing there?" he smiled. "Get in here."

"How can I help?" Nora asked starting forward.

"Well," Aunt Lil said, "you could either take a seat and rest or set the table. It's up to you."

Nora began reacquainting herself with their cupboards.

As always, they'd prepared a lovely supper: a colorful, green salad, roast beef, garlic mashed potatoes and hot biscuits. As they were talking and eating, recollections of childhood Christmases flooded Nora like brightly colored snapshots. Christmas at Lil's had always been special. The house was always amazingly decorated with porcelain nativity figurines, colorfully wrapped presents beneath invariably huge trees and candles beyond compare. Outside, lights like heaven's stars reflected upon the snow. It was nearly impossible for Nora to believe that she'd once lived just down the street.

For dessert, Lil brought out chocolate cake with vanilla ice cream and a chocolate sauce that hardened when it hit the cold treat. After they'd done the dishes, they went into the living room. Nora and Lil settled onto the burgundy velvet couch as Gerry eased into his old recliner. Alternately gazing into the fireplace and at each other, they spoke of Nora's mother, her two brothers and Nora's experiences. "The only thing I liked about California," Nora summed up, "was beautician's school and work. Everything else was awful." Nora gave herself credit for not breaking down again.

"What about your writing?" Gerry asked.

"Oh, there was always writing," Nora smiled. "It's so much a part of me I forget to mention it. And it doesn't really make me *happy*; it just feels like I can't stop, like it's something I have to do."

"I'd like to read some," Gerry said.

"Oh no!" Nora exclaimed. "It's all about sadness, all very schoolgirl."

Gerry moved on, "Are you ready to work with your Aunt Lil?"

"I think so."

"Did you go over the study materials I sent?" Lil asked.

"Of course. I think I'm ready. I'm a pretty good beautician. Thank you so much for offering me a job, Auntie Lil. I was going crazy in Crestline."

"You're welcome, honey. Now, I know we've covered this, but you understand that I can't let you work on clients until you get your New York licenses?"

"Of course, Auntie. I can't believe you got me into a class on such short notice. It starts next week, right?"

"Yes, dear."

"I sure hope I find work soon. I don't want to be a burden on you for long."

"Don't worry about that, hon," Lil said. "We'd like you to stay as long as you'd like. Permanently would be my preference."

"How about if she enrolls in your next desairology class, too?" Gerry butted in. "I mean, if she gets her hair and nails licenses, won't desairology increase her prospects?"

Nora hid her alarm by joking, "Trying to get rid of me already, Uncle?"

"Not at all, my dear. Or not that I'll admit. But didn't you just say you wanted work?"

"That's a great idea!" Lil exclaimed. "I know so many funeral home directors! I could easily find work for you. I'm in the middle of teaching a class right now, but I have another in May."

Uncomfortably, Nora laughed, "Me!? Gosh no! I can't even watch a scary movie! How could I do makeup on dead people?"

"It's not as bad as you might think," Lil said. "Besides, it may take you a while to build up a client base and this would be an immediate opportunity! You should at least try it."

Thinking they'd been plotting this, Nora said, "I don't know, Aunt Lil. Funerals scare me."

"You shouldn't be afraid of them, dear. Believe me, you're much safer at a funeral home than on the streets of L.A. or Brooklyn."

Gerry crossed his ankles and sipped his coffee before saying, "Let's face it, the living are spookier than the dead. Plus, your customers can't talk back. Heh. Or not usually they don't. Right, Lil? Heh."

"I don't know," Nora responded. "Even the sight of blood frightens me. Any time I go for a blood test, I have to look away. I can't even watch blood being drawn from another person without getting dizzy."

"Then this is a good opportunity to conquer your fears," Gerry suggested. "Death finds us all. Who knows? Such work might even make you more appreciative of life."

"Besides," Aunt Lil chimed in, "when you do makeup on the deceased, you won't see any blood, not if they're already embalmed."

"What exactly is embalming?" Nora asked. "I mean, I get that you have to..."

"It's the process of sanitizing, preserving, and restoring a deceased body to a more life-like appearance."

"Yuck. Is that what you do?"

"No, honey, I don't embalm people, I..."

"But you know how it's done?"

"Certainly. A pump is inserted in the carotid artery. Then, when the blood is drained..."

"Oh my God! Stop! Shouldn't that be done at a hospital?"

"No honey, if a hospital does it, they may be trying to cover up some malfeasance. Embalming is done at funeral homes."

"I'm willing to do almost any job," Nora said, "but I'm not sure I could work on corpses!"

Gerry laughed then said, "If you knew how to embalm, you'd have a guaranteed income. But in most states and countries, embalming requires a license. All Lil would teach you is makeup, desairology."

Nora asked, "Who invented this embalming idea? Why don't people just bury the dead right away without makeup or embalming?"

"That's how Muslims handle their deceased," Gerry said. "But, as to embalming, I think the Egyptians were the first who practiced it."

"Don't misunderstand us," Lil remarked, "desairology isn't for everyone. But this nonsense that people feel about death is really quite silly. We have to look at death not with fear but as the end of something precious that God has granted. We should take more counsel from our faiths than our fears."

Nora wished they'd drop the subject. But Lil was still talking, describing the job as nearly as beautiful as doing make up on a bride. "Don't be scared," she said. "Strip away some of what you've been taught. Believing sometimes flies in the face of knowing. I've devoted so much of my life to serving the dead without giving a thought to fear. I'm making a contribution by helping the deceased look as good as they did in life, or better."

"Where do you find the courage?" Nora asked.

Lil smiled. "I don't know that it's courage. It just never bothered me. I've been a beautician for over thirty years, but I remember when I first knew I wanted to work with the deceased. When your grandmother died, your mother, Aunt Edna, Aunt Dolly and I just couldn't believe what they'd done to her! Her hair was combed the opposite way she wore it and she had on bright red lipstick and horrifying rouge. She looked like a scary clown! It really bothered us. 'Who is this woman?' we asked each other. 'Where is our mother?'

"Not long after that, I decided to do makeup on the deceased. Most families could care less about desairology, unless they take a last glimpse at Aunt Mary or Uncle George and discover that their loved one looks like a stranger. It's a horrible thing to experience at a funeral."

"Do you have any students my age?" Nora asked.

"Of course!" Lil beamed. "My younger students are usually less comfortable than the older ones. The more mature students consider desairology to be a service they can proudly provide."

"What are the risks?" Nora asked.

"I can't think of any," Lil said. "I'm tempted to say none, but you never know. I've never come to any harm."

"Are they sitting up or lying down when you work on them?"

"Lying down."

"Do you dress them?"

"Yes, most of the time two of us will handle that. Unless the person is a child, then one of us may..."

"Is dead hair harder to work with than a living person's?"

"Yes, there's no life in the hair, no natural oil."

"If the person was murdered or in a terrible accident, isn't it scary?"

"Again, it depends on who you are. Not for me. If there's significant damage, we simply do what we can. In such cases the caskets are usually closed anyway."

"You said they don't bleed?"

"If they haven't been embalmed, yes. If embalmed, no; but we only work on the embalmed."

"Even the idea terrifies me," Nora said.

"It's difficult to change people's minds if they're already formed about something," Gerry chimed in. "This holds true with death. It's usually about what family or culture we grew up in. Consider the Amman Namgai, a people of New Guinea's swampy southwest coast, one of the world's least visited corners. In many Amman Namgai houses, people wear the skulls of their parents as necklaces in order to frighten off ghosts. The skull of an enemy often serves as a pillow and they may keep half a dozen skulls hanging from their rafters."

"Gross!"

"Oh, I don't know. They polish the skulls so constantly that the bones acquire the sheen of old ivory. In some ways, the fixtures are less gross than immaculate. Babies sleep beside their ancestors' skulls as peacefully as they would beside a Teddy Bear. The Amman Namgai may fear the ghosts of their enemies, but they certainly don't fear what the ghosts have evacuated!"

Nora scowled. Lil shook her head. Nora marveled that such practices could still exist. "How could they keep skulls?" she asked in wonderment. "How could they sleep on them and hang them around their necks?"

"And that's not all," Librarian Gerry explained. "They wear human vertebrae as necklaces and fashion daggers, nose ornaments and harpoons from human bones!"

"Cut it out, Gerry!" Lil said. "It's Nora's first night here. She doesn't need to hear all this! Did you bring up desairology just to frighten her off?"

"Maybe," Uncle Gerry answered. "I don't know. No. But this is where it all starts, in the home. It's how we raise our children. One man's pillow is another's skull. It's all about the mind and how it forms! A joy to the one is a nightmare to another. That's how it is! That's how it'll be forever."

"So, Aunt Lil," Nora asked, "will you teach me to make skull necklaces?"

"That's the spirit!" Gerry exclaimed.

"Oh Gerry," Lil put in, "now look what you've started."

Just then, the wall clock struck midnight. They'd been so immersed in conversation that they'd failed to note the time.

"Well ladies," Gerry said while rising, "it looks like its bedtime. Can I get either of you a skull pillow?"

"Stop it, Gerry!" Lil pleaded.

Before saying goodnight, Nora hugged Gerry and Lil again. She thanked them for their generosity in helping a confused, desperate niece. Then, more reluctantly, she said, "I'll think about your desairology class, Aunt Lil."

"Feel free to sit in on my ongoing class if you'd like. It might allay some of your concerns. We resume tomorrow night."

Seeing Nora's uncertain expression, Lil went on, "Just sleep on it. We didn't mean to pressure or frighten you. We just want to broaden your options."

"*I* wanted to frighten her," Gerry clarified.

"Please ignore the bookish old coot," Lil recommended. "Have a sweet and peaceful night, honey."

"I'll try," Nora said. "You too."

In her room, Nora sat on the edge of her bed and prayed her regular prayer: "Dear Lord, please give Dennis Pino a lesson before he leaves this earth. Maybe send him to New Guinea and hang his skull from a rafter. Or worse. Amen."

Nora went to bed but couldn't sleep. Staring at the ceiling and windows, she wondered what to do. She had to earn some money. She didn't want to be a burden on her aunt and uncle for long. 'I'm here,' she thought. 'I need to figure out what's next. I need to make things happen. Desairology is available. Maybe that's what I should do. If Lil's willing to help, how could I refuse? She's so strong in areas where I'm weak. I should try desairology. If it's too much, I'll quit. It's worth a try.'

She was certainly grateful and yet hesitant. Despite all the talk about death and fear and the images of skulls resting on ivory white bedspreads, and of vertebrae swinging on strings around someone's neck, she slept peacefully.

Open Up those Golden Gates…

Nora was born in Brooklyn in 1966, the first child of three to Art and Lorna Wheeler. New York was a wonderful place during Nora's early years; it suited her perfectly. But when she was twelve, everything shifted. Nora's father had invested all the family's money, including a sizeable inheritance from his parents, in a leading New York financial firm, Pino Capital Trust, one Wall Street's top market outfits. Dennis Pino was the owner and founder of this firm that functioned as a third market provider.

In the seventies, following months of investigation, federal agents charged Mr. Pino with running one of the largest securities frauds in Wall Street's history. After his arrest, Mr. Pino told investigators that he was "financially finished," that he had "absolutely nothing left." He admitted that the essence of his scheme had been to deposit clients' money into a bank, rather than invest it and generate the gigantic returns he claimed. He also confessed to having spent most of his clients' money on mansions, villas, jets, cars, boats and jewelry for himself, his wife and children.

To avoid naming coconspirators, including most of his family, Pino pled guilty to seventeen federal felonies, including money laundering, securities fraud, mail fraud, wire fraud, bribery and attempted bribery of financial officers, perjury, theft from employee benefit plans, including teacher and firefighter retirement funds, and making false filings with the SEC. Mr. Pino suggested that, if not for a single young agent's persistence, no one would have found out about his scam until he died.

Although Pino's lawyers originally asked the judge to impose a sentence of ten years owing to Pino's age and fragile health, the judge handed down the maximum sentence of one hundred years. Pino's wife and children broke their silence after the trial, insisting that they'd never had anything to do with the fraud. Few believed them, certainly not Nora and her family.

Nora would never forget the awful day, early in the Pino investigation, when her father brought his news home from the office. As he entered the kitchen where Nora was helping her mother, she'd never seen him look so harried. He seemed both nervous and sad, something she had never observed in him before.

"Art," Nora's mother asked right away, "what is it? What's wrong?"

"Everything's gone, Lorna. Everything. We have our savings account left. That's all."

Immediately, Nora's mother's beautiful face transformed. Her mouth quivered and her eyes glared. Nora had never seen anything like it before. She bit her lower lip. Tears were already starting. "It can't be," her mother protested. "You said, you said..."

Shaking his head, Nora's father answered, "It is. I didn't tell you everything. I couldn't. We..."

Her frugal mother went nuts. "What are we going to *do*?!" she screamed.

Nora, uncertain what was happening, was glad that her brothers were already sleeping. She had a big lump in her throat and tears in her eyes. Staring at the floor, she was completely uncertain what to do or say. At this point Nora's father awakened to his daughter's presence. "Nora honey, please go to your room. Your mother and I need to..."

"Why?" Nora cried. "What's happening?"

"Please honey," he repeated, "just go to your room."

Reluctantly, Nora left. But she didn't go far. As her parents resumed their shouting she sat on the stairs and listened. They sounded like lunatics, her mother especially. "Answer me!" her mother shrilled. "*What* will we do?!"

Nora had heard her parents argue before, but never like this.

"I guess some praying couldn't hurt."

"Are you *delusional*?! Are you *insane*?! *Pray*?!"

"I've tried everything else."

"It was your *greed*," Nora's mother wailed. "How could you invest everything we had in one single... I don't even know what to call it! I *told* you. I told you this would…"

"I'm not greedy. I..."

"Do you remember what I *told* you?! Do you remember what you *said*?!"

"I..."

"'God intended us to *prosper*!' you said. How could you have been so naïve? No, not naïve, *stupid*! Only an idiot would have...!"

34

"I am *not* an idiot!" her father shouted for the first time. "Since when must everything be easily or logically explained? We've been dealt a hard blow. Now we'll have to weather it! We'll either float together or be torn apart and drown! Do you think that belittling me is going to *help*?!"

"What do you expect me to *say*?! Oh my God! Oh my God! I can't believe I let you…"

"I have my degree. We *both* do. I'll start looking for a full-time job tomorrow."

"You haven't practiced journalism since college! Even then you treated it like it was… like it was…"

"You should start looking too."

"I can't believe you *kept* this from me! You *knew*! You *knew* this was coming!"

"I knew it was a possibility, hon, not that…"

"Don't you *hon* me, you liar! You *liar*!"

At this point, Nora, weeping as if her world was collapsing, finally retreated to her bedroom. With the sound downstairs reduced to a very adamant murmur, she huddled in her room's deepest corner. The ensuing days seemed like hell to her. She had no idea it'd be so for years.

***

It took over a month for her father to get a job offer, but when the Star Gazette Newspaper in Riverside, California presented him with a reporter's position, he seized it immediately. The day her father announced they were moving what remained of Nora's foundation crumbled. It broke her heart to think of leaving their home, extended family and friends.

As they drove across the country, Nora continuously listened to her Walkman playing, *Leaving on a Jet Plane*. Despite her younger brothers' ridicule and her parents' entreaties, she wept silently for hours each day throughout the trip. Except for her oldest uncle, Earl, who was working for the Gazette, they hardly knew anyone in California. Nora recalled how, during a visit they'd paid Uncle Earl a couple years earlier, her father had been so smitten by the huge homes near Sunset Boulevard and in Beverly Hills. She remembered how he openly fantasized about owning one of those huge estates.

***

Her father worked for the newspaper for less than two years. He was by far their oldest cub reporter and seemed unable to concentrate on his assignments. Her parents had never been the same since New York, but when Nora's father lost his job, things hit rock bottom. Their mortgage payments piled up until the bank took their home. When even their humble attempts at rebuilding wilted, Uncle Earl helped them to find the cheapest accommodations possible in the small, San Bernardino mountain town of Crestline. All five family members were soon piled into a primitive cabin. The tiny house's greatest attributes were its windows and screened-in front porch, all of which framed landscapes of the forest and hills curving against the sky. There were three puny bedrooms, one bathroom and a dining-living room rolled into one. The kitchen was like a closet.

Nora's father, tall and skinny with brown hair graying at the temples, had come to look like a completely barren soul. It seemed that all of his once vast ambitions had been crushed out of him. His sad brown eyes seemed forever lost. Her mother harangued Art about their situation almost daily. Before the family's fall, Art was always dreaming of becoming, not just upper-middle-class, but downright rich. One of his greatest dreams had always been to take his family traveling around the world. Now, working with a tree trimming and yard cleanup service, he felt he'd never reacquire even the dream of such things.

Nora had hated Southern California since their arrival, but the mountains were even worse. Not only was it boring, but she had to hike nearly two miles to get to the main highway for the school bus each morning. She wore tattered white tennis shoes every day, even when the snow came. A few kids at Rim of the World High School heckled her daily. Although she was a good student, it was hard to be the new girl, especially when she was considered poor. Others shared her economic tier, but she didn't reach out to them either.

Most of the kids had nice clothes and extra money. She ate lunch alone. Nora always felt lonely and that she was an outsider. She was not invited to parties. Soon she had trouble getting along with the students and teachers. Her brothers, being only a year apart and still in grade school, had each other and fared far better. Nora was hurt but never told her parents how much she felt their poverty, struggles and disappointments. She wouldn't let them know she was suffering.

Despite all this, she grew closer to her dad in Crestline. It just felt like they were suffering the most. Not everything was unadulterated gloom. Some early fall nights were cozy in the cabin. Her father read his latest short stories to them as her mother, who would still smile occasionally, knitted woolen sweaters and scarves.

In November of 1980, Art's job came to its seasonal end. If he didn't find work soon the family wouldn't be able to make rent. Her mother's employment as a maid for a vacation rental outfit brought in less than half of what they needed. A few days before Thanksgiving, Nora looked out the living room window to see her father sitting on their tiny front porch; smoking, he looked dejected and depressed. Mr. Horton, their nearest neighbor, was passing by, walking his two golden retrievers. "Dreaming, Art?" he called.

"Not so much dreaming as pondering the mystery of it all."

"Mystery of what?"

"Why something that gave us the power to dream doesn't give us the power to realize."

Mr. Horton stared for a moment. "There's no mystery about that, Art. It does. Quit dreaming so much and get to work is all. You'll soon get what you want."

"Untrue, Mr. Horton You're a successful man. I'm a complete failure. Our perspectives will never align."

"Then how do you account for my success? Heck, what about the success of all men who've applied the same method?"

"What method?"

"I just told you. Work. And then work some more."

"I can't agree," Nora's father said. "Your blueprint doesn't fit my case, or the case of thousands like me. No one has worked harder than me, but I have nothing left. I've accomplished nothing. In the eyes of my family, friends, and successful men, I *am* nothing."

"You've been up here for only a few months, Art. I've seen that you have a great work ethic. If you've worked just as faithfully all your life, I can't understand why you're not a great success today."

Exhaling a grey cloud, Art shrugged. "I just don't know Mr. Horton. Fate? The planets? You tell me. Of course, hard work's necessary. And, believe it or not, there are few things that I love more; but there *must be* something else. If work ethic was everything, I'd be a millionaire."

"It isn't too late. You have still time. There's plenty of time and hope for everybody."

"*That* is completely ludicrous. *Everyone* has a shot? Ridiculous. Plenty of time? Time is death. Hope? Nine times out of ten, hope is a complete impostor."

"Supposing they are? What else can you do? Give up? Just keep at it. One of these days things will turn."

"I *have been* hard at it for over twenty years! Here are the results." Art waved at the surroundings. "I'm so *sick* of the futility. Jesus Christ, where do ambitions and desires even originate? There must be someone who knows. If I could discover ambition's source… If I could discern *that*, would it make my ambitions… more *understandable*? Maybe even more *realizable*?"

"You're going into the mystery rather deeply, aren't you, Art? In a way, I admire your wanting to get to rock bottom, but don't become a mystical philosopher."

"What do you mean by mystical, Mr. Horton? Are you referring to fairies or the likes of Meister Eckhardt and Teresa of Avila?"

"I don't know, Art. Personally, I think very little of the man who simply speculates. My ideal is of action."

"We agree, Mr. Horton. I *want* to do things. But what is the scope? Did *you* orchestrate your birth and culture? Do you know how many hairs clutter your head? Whatever power manages such things can answer the how and whys of my... accursed ambitions."

"Enough philosophy for the moment. You look like a ghost, Art. What's really the matter?"

Art was quiet for some seconds. Nora couldn't see his expression, but she thought she felt the appearance, or return of something very cold. "Everything's gone," Art muttered. "Nothing's left. They're going to turn off the heat. We won't even be to make rent."

"Art," Mr. Horton asked, "how much do you need?"

"So I'm a beggar now. This is what it's come to."

"Stop it," Mr. Horton said. "Everyone goes through... How much?"

"It doesn't matter."

Looking grave, Mr. Horton left. Unnoticed, Nora watched her father. Bob Horton was back within minutes, handing a check to Art.

Gazing at it, Art said, "I appreciate this, Bob. Thank you. But I don't know when I'll be able to repay you."

Mr. Horton, gripping Art's shoulder, said, "Look, Art, I don't care. Consider it a gift. I've been where you are, believe me." Mr. Horton noticed Nora. "Nora, things won't always be like this, but remember this day. There'll be times when someone needs your help. If you do what you can for them, that'll be my repayment. Happy Thanksgiving."

As Art turned and stared at Nora, realizing she'd overheard the entire exchange, she started weeping. "I… Mr. Horton began. But he didn't finish. He set off down the path again. Art came inside.

Glancing at Nora, he seemed miles away. "There must be an answer," he muttered. "I'll find it. Things can't go on like... I resolve to clear the… Even though I should perish. My mind is made up. A life that can't satisfy a single desire has no..."

He seemed completely unhinged. Nora couldn't even decide if he was speaking to her or himself. Witnessing his agitated state, she was very relieved that her brothers and mother were out.

Art was still raving: "Nothing can live in vain, even though existence should be a little more than a barren waste. To think otherwise is to contradict nature and reason. I have wife and… But why do I desire things I can't realize? Why desire the rare, the rich, the beautiful, the sublime? To make one hungry and not give the means to… It's cruelty. And yet something is... And the future? Will I realize the ruling ambitions, will I find it?"

Unable to decide whether the raving question had been rhetorical or not, Nora simply kept weeping. Art turned and went back outside. Nora watched him disappear into the woods. When her mother and brothers came home, Nora said she didn't know where he'd gone. He didn't come back until dinner.

That night Art seemed to be two personalities, the one proceeding mechanically and the other pondering, as if in another world, what the outcome of his new resolution would be. Neither Nora nor Art mentioned the strange afternoon. That night, in keeping with his regular habits, Art offered an affectionate "Goodnight" to his three children, and then went to bed.

***

On Thanksgiving morning, Art, Lorna, and their children drove down the mountain to visit Uncle Earl's family. Heavy, ominous clouds stormed across the sky as the family drove down the narrow, winding highway.

Art had been pretty much lucid since Nora had seen his mind bend, but she could still sense his depression tearing at him. She couldn't look at him without trying to occupy his very being. Why, she imagined him wondering, had he ever left New York? He was then thinking about his comfortable youth, or aspects he'd mentioned to her. He was wishing for his mother's embrace, contemplating his father's hand upon his shoulder, yearning to relive conversations with his cousins once more. Then he was back in the present, or nearly, longing to enjoy Thanksgivings without being so beset by worry.

Heavy raindrops began assaulting the windshield. The wipers came on. Art, Nora surmised, was fighting back tears as the silently drove. By the time they reached Riverside, Earl's front lawn had become a vast puddle. The family made their way up the front walk. Art knocked.

The door swung open. Art was beaming. "Welcome!" he nearly shouted. Happy Thanksgiving!"

"Yeah!" Nora's brothers responded, hugging their uncle.

"Get in there, boys!" he said, brushing them indoors.

Less ebullient greetings followed. Nora envied her brothers' sweet ignorance. They all entered the house. The scent of roasting turkey filled the home. "Why don't you guys head to the game room?" Earl directed the children.

Trailing her scampering brothers and cousins, Nora had no interest in being around them. They were all so damn oblivious to everything. After watching scrambling, celebratory youth disappear through the game-room door, Nora pressed her back against the hallway wall then slid down to a seated position. From her right, the sounds of lunatic kids dominated. From her left, adults worshipped other illusions.

Scarlet, Earl's wife, was saying, "Would you help me in the kitchen, Lorna?"

"Of course," Nora's mother answered.

Peeking around a doorframe, Nora saw Earl and Art heading for the living room. She followed them. Sitting just outside the men's lair, she stole another quick glance around another doorframe. Art was in a chair near the fireplace, gazing into the flames as Art jabbed the blaze with a skinny oak log. He laid the piece upon the fire. "How is everything, Art?" Earl said.

"Pretty awful," Art responded.

Nora stretched out on her belly and resumed

"Any word on those jobs you applied for?" Earl asked.

"No! Nothing! I'm sick of achieving nothing. I'm sick of getting my hopes crushed over and over. I'm a tired, broke loser." He sunk his head into his hands.

Earl looked sympathetic. "Art, I know you're going through a rough spell, and I can't imagine how difficult is, but hardships are a big part of life. You're harping on misfortune and magnifying the negativity. Try to take a step back for a little perspective."

Art looked up. "If you knew *anything*, you'd know... life hasn't been just with me."

"Look, Art, I know the head editor of the Lake Arrowhead Golden Bear. It's a small town paper, but... I'll ask him to give you a job if you're interested."

"I don't know," Art muttered. He shut his eyes for a second or two, and then reopened them. "Not yet."

"For Christ's sake Art, if you're just going to dismiss help when it..." Earl paused. "Today's Thanksgiving. We should count our blessings."

"My life doesn't feel blessed right now," Art moaned.

"Jesus, Art, buck up. How can someone with such a beautiful family even *think* such a thing? If your life doesn't seem worthwhile, focus more on all you've accomplished and less on what's been taken. Start with gratitude or worse things will befall you."

"Be thankful for His blessings?!" Art mocked. "No, I can't I can't pray that way. Your words are all Hallmark clichés."

"They're not," Earl lectured. "Have you ever tried meditating?"

"Give me a break. I'm drowning and you tell me to meditate. I don't have the patience."

"Well, you'd better find it then. There's no serenity in you right now. How do you expect to come out of this tailspin if you won't… You have to relax. You need to forget what you think of yourself. Make no effort to be quiet; just feel quiet; and aim to be calm and still. Nature must be given the opportunity to restore equilibrium."

"It's easy for you to say, Earl, but…I…"

Earl interrupted, "When your mind is at rest, the day-to-day problems temporarily disappear. When they return, they can be more easily understood. Consider your troubles an invitation to experience."

Art wasn't having it. "You don't get it, do you? There's nothing to be done. The hole's too deep. I've failed."

Earl looked worried. "What are you saying, Art? If you need help, you know I'm here, right?"

"I don't need your money." Art stood up and put more wood on the fire. He held his hands to the warmth.

Earl put his right arm on Art's shoulder. "If you ever need anything, don't hesitate to ask. I'm always here to support you."

"Certainly." Art stared at the fire.

"Nora!" Lorna called from the kitchen.

Panicked, Nora drew her spying head back from the doorframe. Fairly certain that the men hadn't seen her, she got up and, as softly as she possibly could, ran toward the kitchen. As she entered, her mother was already holding a two-foot beaten tine tray spread with crackers, cheese and cut apples. Immediately, she offered it to Nora. "Take this to your uncle and father."

Without a word, Nora received her chore. "Pino will pay. That thief ruined me!" Art was nearly shouting as Nora made her way back to the men. "I won't rest until he's screaming in hell!"

As Nora appeared in the doorway, Art was pointing to his own chest and scowling as if all his reason had fled. Seeing his daughter, he shook off some of his rage. "Hello, honey," Earl said.

"Mom told me to bring these," she said, lifting the tray a trifle higher.

"That's nice of you, sweetie," her father said.

She entered then set the food on a coffee table. The men thanked her then stared until she grew uncomfortable. "OK," she said, walking out. Of course, as soon as she turned into the hallway, she froze.

"Art," Earl resumed, "you blame others too much. It was your decision to invest with Pino, even against all warnings. Have you accepted even *partial* responsibility? Look at the whole situation, not just the effects!"

The room became quiet. Nora could sense how annoyed Art must've been. This was their first family Thanksgiving in years.

"Don't you care?" Earl asked.

"Care?" Art asked. "Care about what?"

"Anything! Your family! Thanksgiving! Don't you care it's Thanksgiving? Doesn't it matter to you?"

"No," Art answered. "Not really. One day's the same as another to me. I know what's expected, though, so here we are."

"You need to knock it off," Earl commanded. "You're like… It's like you've become addicted to bitterness and self-pity. Your family matters. Taking care of them and their future matters. *This day* matters. Your moping doesn't matter. Your anger doesn't matter. Your money or lack of it, just doesn't matter!"

The room went quiet. Nora was thinking about leaving when Earl resumed,

"Move on, Art. Gather yourself and try harder. Ultimately, you'll thrive. I can't help but believe that. It'll be hard, but you'll solve it."

"OK," Art said. "I've heard everything you've said. I'm pissed and hate every crap word of it and will do my best to make your predictions accurate. Now, can we please watch the freaking game?"

"Sure," Earl said.

Hearing the TV come on, Nora returned to the kitchen. Her mother and Scarlett put her to work, mashing potatoes and assaulting vegetables. Unengaged, she was bored. But the day continued. Art managed to conceal most of his depressed fury. After dinner, he actually seemed a bit happier. He even floated some jokes. A little past eight, it was time to leave.

"Good night," Art said, hugging Earl. "Thanks for your patience today. I did hear you."

"I'm glad we did this, thanks for coming. You can do it."

They all continued down the driveway. Art, Lorna and their children got into their car. Waving, they left. Driving back home, Nora wondered if Art was considering the Lake Arrowhead newspaper job. He seemed calmer, she thought. 'If he'd just take the job,' she thought, 'things might be alright.'

***

It was Sunday, a week before Christmas. The bright sun was reflecting off a fresh dusting of snow. Nora and her brothers were throwing powdery snowballs amidst the front yard's pine trees and laughing hysterically when the cabin's front door flew open. Her mother burst out onto the porch, trembling and looking impossibly frightened. In a wispy, frantic voice she called, "Nora, take your brothers to the Horton's. Then come right back."

"Why?" Nora asked.

Lorna gave her a look like she wanted to break her legs. "Just take them, *now*! And come back immediately!"

"Let's go," Nora told her brothers. She took their hands. As she led them across the quarter mile to the Horton's, she thought over and over, 'Something terrible has happened.'

She left the boys with Mrs. Horton then ran back home. The porch's metal-framed screen door banged shut behind her. She burst into the living room. Her mother was sitting on the tattered couch, crying somehow quietly but hysterically. Her heart was beating like a jackhammer as Nora walked over. "Mom, what's wrong?!" she cried. "What's going on?!"

"Come here, Nora," Lorna sobbed. "Sit down." She patted the couch.

A stagnant gloom owned the room. Nora sat, thinking she was about to receive terrible news. Her mother patted Nora's back as tears streamed down her face. Trembling, she said, "Honey, it's... I don't know how to tell you."

"What, Mom?"

"It's your dad, honey."

Nora, however much she'd already suspected this, was frozen. Her mother's eyes were swollen and bloodshot, her complexion ghostly pale, her body shaking uncontrollably. Feebly, she gestured toward the back window. Staring, Nora said, "Oh no, no!" It was her first reaction. Nora didn't know what else to do. Her dad, hanging under the backyard's largest and most beautiful oak, was swinging gently. It was a mighty tree, five feet in diameter, with thick limbs thrust out in all directions.

Neither Nora nor her mother rose. She couldn't believe what she was seeing. Complete dread had overtaken her. It couldn't be real. Then Lorna, still weeping, was hugging her. They both wept as if the world was ending. Then her mother was rising, pulling Nora's hand, leading her. They walked out back and, a few feet from the stately tree, simply stared. Nora stood there, stunned. "What do we do?" she eventually pleaded.

Her mother remained silent for some seconds, then, "Call someone, honey. I haven't…"

"Okay, Mom."

Nora ran in and dialed 911. It took all the strength she had.

"911, what is your emergency?"

Her words seemed to run away from her. She was too panicked to catch them. She began, "My, my father, hanging." She stopped. Her mouth trembled; her face collapsed into tears.

"I'm sorry," the operator or dispatcher was saying, "Are you there? I didn't understand."

"My father," Nora blurted. "It's my father…he…he hanged himself. We need help…"

The conversation seemed like a dream. The dispatcher kept her on the phone until the first sheriff arrived. Before long a swarm of sheriff's deputies and firefighters overran the property. Then the coroner came. Then her dad was gone. She went to the Horton's and brought her brothers home.

In the ensuing days, Lorna's siblings rallied around the mourning family, both brothers and her three sisters. Other family members and friends came from all over the country to attend Art's funeral. But Aunt Lil and Uncle Gerry were the bulwarks. If they hadn't flown out from New York, and spent a month with Lorna and her kids, who knows what might've happened?

Nora couldn't sleep for weeks. Throughout many long dark evenings, as her two brothers and her mother slept, Nora lay awake, tainted with fear in awful stillness. She wept in secret and, raising her streaming eyes to her bedroom's windows, saw the image of her father's body, hanging on the oak tree. Then she'd see her father's coffin being lowered into the earth, disappearing as attendants stood ready with their shovels and the minister read prayers.

Many nights, long after everyone was sleeping, Nora would go to the living room to sit on their tired couch and stare at the oak.

The icy moon glowed on the snow, but refused to light her world. Their house, set so far back from the road, now seemed astoundingly eerie. Every night, she wondered, 'How did everything fall to such misery?' Her constant encounters with the past begat a chronic melancholy.

After the Christmas holidays, when school started, Nora dutifully attended. She was extremely sensitive about her dad's death. It was hard to be in school and deal with numerous rumors about her dad's suicide. Nora, while she never felt she'd fit in at Rim of the World, had always been a good student and had perfect attendance. Now everything unraveled. It seemed there was nothing she could do to improve her life; that the downward spiral would continue forever. She had trouble concentrating and began skipping class. She'd begun to hate school. Instead of going, she would stay home at least two days a week and try to study literature, history, and art on her own. Lil, Gerry and Nora's mom protested only a little. Nora didn't care to find a boyfriend. She only cared about writing. It felt like the only outlet she had.

After Lil and Gerry left, Lorna and her three children had no support. For weeks, Nora's mother was too devastated to do anything but go to work. Finally, after two months, she applied for welfare. They got on the dole but it wasn't enough. As a sideline, she began cleaning private homes in Lake Arrowhead. She was the first person up in the morning and the last to bed at night. Finally, after a long search, Nora found a part-time, after-school work at Dove Beauty Salon in Crestline, cleaning and sweeping the floors.

Because money was so tight, Nora and her brothers wore clothing from the local thrift stores or whatever throwaways her mother could find. At least they still had her father's old car. If the car was running and they had gas money, they scavenged. Lorna would drive while Nora walked hunting through trashcans for anything of value.

One day, when a classmate was making fun of her threadbare clothing and asking, "Isn't your mom a maid?" Nora hauled off and punched the girl. She was suspended for a week. After returning to school, she didn't speak with anyone, not even her teachers. The next month, she refused to go at all. She was seventeen when she quit high school. Nora took classes at a beauty college down in San Bernardino. Every day, she went down the mountain. After a year, she got her cosmetology license. Just after her nineteenth birthday,

she started working as a beautician in Crestline's *Dove Salon*.

## Meanwhile, Back in Brooklyn

Nora awoke stiff and weary. The scent of coffee and bacon wafted through the bedroom. She showered and dressed. Then, with her hair in a ponytail, she descended the steep, narrow stairway. Lil and Gerry were in the kitchen. Gerry, wearing a gray suit, stood at the kitchen table. Lil wore a nice dress under a full pink apron with crisscross straps neatly tied in back. They looked like a carefree, happy couple.

Seeing Nora, Lil said, "Good morning, honey. Did you sleep well?"

"Yes, very," Nora said, cheerfully.

"How many eggs would you like?"

"One would be fine."

"You'll have two."

Their making her breakfast made Nora feel like the most important person in the world. She loved watching her aunt work. When they'd offered thanks for the bacon, eggs, oatmeal and coffee, Nora said, "I've decided to take your desairology class, Aunt Lil. And I know I've said this already, or wrote it, but I'd like to help as much as I can at your salon and around here too."

"I'm so glad to hear that, Nora," Lil responded.

"Me too." Gerry added.

After eating, Gerry set out for the library. Not long afterwards, Lil and Nora walked to the nearby salon. As Lil turned on the lights and opened the blinds, Nora strolled about, reabsorbing the familiar place. Lil's salon flooded Nora with more childhood memories. Before her family fled to California, Nora had whiled away so many happy hours there with her cousins. Except for the sharp odor of permanent solution, she'd loved everything about the place.

Back then, Lil was never too preoccupied to spend time with Nora and her cousins. She enjoyed having the young girls visit her booming business. The small establishment—always a place for women to gossip and talk about husbands, children, boyfriends, and current events—had afforded Nora and her cousins a sort of haven, even when they hadn't really needed one.

The VIP cups still filled their designated shelves, bearing the names of regular customers. Even if a patron had passed, her sparkling clean cup remained as a sort of tribute. Three other beauticians worked in the salon, but many clients would wait up to a month for Lil. Being one of her regulars brought a certain local status.

Shortly before nine, the other stylists entered. Then customers began arriving. While sweeping and cleaning, Nora sorted through emotions. As Lil and the other beauticians worked, Nora recalled standing on the sidewalk outside her cousins' home so many years ago, calling out for them. When they came out they'd all traipse down the block to Lil's salon. They all loved spending time there.

The dark burgundy leather chairs had been like thrones to them. The girls would spin squealing until Lil laughingly stopped their antics. Some of the older customers weren't overly fond of children cavorting about; but if they wanted Lil's services, they had to put up with it. The smell of perm solution and hair color stung their eyes and burned their nostrils. There were always piles of hair on the floor, brown, black, gray and blond, some straight and some curly. Drawers and metal carts afforded hairbrushes, combs, scissors, and rollers of various sizes and colors: bright pink, green, blue and beige.

Nora remembered how Lil—young, beautiful, tall and slim in those days—stood regally straight in her black apron, diligently snapping her scissors. One of Lil's favorite hairbrushes back then had a hot pink, see-through plastic handle. For no reason she could think of, the instrument had fascinated young Nora. After Lil reined them in Nora and her cousins would retreat to a corner to chat, pop bubblegum and burst into giggling fits. What wonderful times they'd had!

In the present, Nora wished she was still that carefree child. The joy of those years now seemed nearly impossible, far more than life afforded. Contrarily, back in those happy, safe years, Nora could hardly wait to be old enough to work beside her aunt.

After making the salon even more immaculate, Nora wandered through a rear door into Lil's classroom behind the shop. In addition to the usual beauty school offerings, the room contained half a dozen tables. On each was a mannequin—male or female, adult or child—with their heads resting on cotton pillows. They'd creeped out Nora and her cousins to no end when they were children. To Nora's chagrin, they still gave her the shivers. She returned out front and set about wiping down the already clean counters.

As five o'clock approached, Lil finished for the day. "Nora honey," she called, "would you like to grab a quick bite before class?"

She nodded. She and her aunt went to a nearby coffee shop for coffee and pastry. As they walked back to Lil's, Nora said, "Why am I so nervous, Aunt Lil?"

"I don't know, honey. Is your dad's funeral the only one you've ever attended?"

"Yes."

"That might explain it."

By six they'd returned to Lil's classroom. The students began arriving and finding their seats shortly before the six-thirty start time. There were ten. To Nora's eyes, some seemed uncomfortable. That night they were dealing with severe cuts and bruises to the face and head. The most squeamish seemed reluctant to utilize the mannequins for what they were: learning tools. Some seemed to be struggling. Watching them, Nora thought she could do better than many, but wasn't sure that she wanted to.

As leery as Nora remained, she was also very impressed with her aunt's teaching. Lil clearly enjoyed interacting with students, making them as comfortable as possible. Nora was still struggling very hard to brush aside feelings of fear and discomfort.

When Nora had spent four days cleaning and observing at Lil's, a Manhattan funeral home called to offer Lil a job. Over dinner that night, Lil asked, "Nora, would you like to come to Manhattan with me tomorrow? I'll have to be there at eight, so we'd have to leave early."

Smiling nervously, Nora said, "I'm not really ready to... Do you mean to...? Only if I don't have to..."

"Oh, you don't have to work with me, dear. You're welcome to watch if you'd like, but feel free to reacquaint yourself with Manhattan until I finish. Afterwards, we could have lunch and just spend some time together, maybe even shop a little."

"That would be lovely, Aunt Lil. I'd love to see Manhattan again. It's been a long time."

"Wonderful! We have a date then."

"How come you kids get all the fun?" Gerry pouted.

"Would you like to come with us, Gerry?" Lil asked.

"I, uh, well. Let's see, I..."

"As I thought," Lil said. "You would no more leave your books to shop than you'd let me dye your hair blue."

"Blue?" Gerry asked. "You've never offered *blue* before. What shade exactly?"

"Your choice, my dear. Go to the paint store and pick out a swatch."

"Heh," Gerry chortled. "*Royal* blue methinks. What else would be suitable for this princely curmudgeon?"

Nora loved their regular badinage. The conversation continued along such nonsensical veins until they finished eating and moved on to dishes. Eventually, they were heading off to bed. That night, a cold front moved in. By the time Nora woke, it was in the low forties outside. After breakfast, Nora and Lil bundled up and said goodbye to Gerry. Then, as dawn broke, they set out for Manhattan. When their subway tram stopped, they picked their way through the busy station toward the stairs. In front of Sam's Deli, Lil said, "I should be done by eleven, if not sooner. Shall we meet back here then?"

"Sure, Aunt Lil."

"Have fun, honey."

"You too. I mean, um..."

Smiling, Aunt Lil walked off.

Nora had hours to wander. At first, she avoided Wall Street. It reminded her too much of loss. But she couldn't stop thinking about it. She felt like a hot-air balloon. Obsessed and feeling she had to get over it, she headed for Wall Street. Arriving at the street sign, memories flooded back. The road was jammed with pedestrians and vendors. Newspapers were for sale, coffee, hot chocolate and so on. Yellow taxis were cutting up and down the avenues. She reflected back upon the many times she'd visited Wall Street with her parents, aunts and uncles. She and her cousins would stroll around munching bags of buttery popcorn, sharing M&Ms and squabbling over colors.

Nora felt nostalgic over such details. In the present, reliving the sights and sounds of her childhood, she was struck by the odd feeling that the setting had shrunk. Surrounded by tall buildings, she paused before the New York Stock Exchange and recalled her first visit there in the spring of 1977. She'd been eleven years old and visiting with her class. That long-ago excursion afforded Nora and her fellow students their first glimpse of how the world economy was so influenced by one institution. Guided by their teacher, Mr. Metz, Nora's class watched from the trading floor's visitor's gallery as the scene below them boiled with energy.

Standing with her classmates, Nora tuned out Mr. Metz's lecture to attend to a nearby man describing the place to his friend, who seemed to be a foreigner. "This stock market is the most capitalistic institution in the world's most capitalist society," the man said. "I consider it a greed engine, a tool for destroying human happiness."

Pointing at the brokers, he continued, "Just look at those lunatics, shilling for capitalism and so-called freedom, the freedom of the already wealthy to profit!" Shaking his head, he'd gone on, "This place is nothing more than a glorified casino, a speculative orgy! I'm actually glad that other societies outlaw such madness."

Nora, hearing such things well before her father's difficulties, was shocked.

The man's friend—a muscular, square-jawed fellow with curly black hair, brown eyes and thick-rimmed glasses—was nodding in agreement. "In my country, we believe that money is best apportioned at the discretion of government." Gazing at the floor, he commented, "In my country, we are horrified by how much of the world's work gets channeled through Wall Street."

"But most Americans," his guide responded, "think your people wait in lines for everything: food, buses, magazines, taxis and movies. Such rationing is often cited here as proof that communism doesn't work."

"In this way, my country guarantees equality; everyone waits. Well, most do. There are no taxes, rents are low and the price of food is reasonable. All education is free and all medical attention, from simple infections to open-heart surgery, are without charge for all. But of course rich people hate that idea!"

Nora, impressed by the trading floor's boiling operations, and knowing about her father's respect for it, was confused by the duo's animosity. Didn't her father make a large part of their family's income from this place? But, as she watched the tumult in the cavernous room—five stories high, 140 feet long and 115 feet wide—she pondered the men's words. When the two men moved on, she tuned back into Mr. Metz's words.

"The rules of the Exchange," Mr. Metz was explaining, "prohibit running." Nora looked. Many brokers, traders, dealers, clerks, messengers and reporters were hurrying from place to place in a sort of panicked penguin's gait. The floor was littered with scrapes of colored paper and pencils. An enormous American flag drooped from a pole set into the north wall, but the dominant figure was the statue of a woman with outstretched arms, the image of *Financial Integrity*.

"Number 11 Wall Street," Mr. Metz was saying, "is the inescapable symbol and temple of our capitalist economy. Just as a shark can't stop swimming, this exchange can't ever cease seeking profit. Common stocks, which are a form of currency, facilitate this searching movement, allowing money to find its way to old and new enterprises. The value of a stock is less fixed than that of a coin; it changes according to what people think of it. A stock market is a continuous auction at which oil, food, medicine, furniture, technology, next year's coffee or what have you, are traded in accordance with what people think of their present and future worth.

"The price of any stock is determined by prevailing opinions. The collective's changing opinions—subject to rumor, dividends, inflation, war, revolutions, fear, hope, whim and greed—is discerned in the price of trades. The trading is handled by a community of brokers, members of the Exchange, who act as agents for those seeking to buy or sell. These middlemen are of all types, but," Mr. Metz smiled, "many suffer from ulcers and undue optimism."

Resurfacing from memory, Nora found herself staring up at the building's main façade: six tall Corinthian columns topped with marble pediments containing high-relief sculptures representing *Integrity Protecting the World of Man*. 'What a place!' she thought. 'Every day, it makes some happy and others suicidal, all driven by at least some degree of gambler instincts.'

Daring not to enter, she walked on, thinking of her family's travails and how the stock market's worst aspects had so changed their lives. She was becoming more downcast with each step. Shuffling along Wall Street, staring at the constant stream of people and traffic, she thought, 'People never give up dreaming of quick riches! Most are so influenced by their pocketbooks. Despite all the corruption, sophisticated obstructions and manipulations, trade goes on and on, with some becoming rich and others getting shattered!"

Sorry she'd come, she walked and walked, barely noticing anything, absorbed in her thinking. As eleven o'clock drew nigh, she was tired and hungry, cold and depressed. She covered the eight blocks back to Sam's Deli and then entered the warm, small restaurant. She watched sandwiches being made. Thin slices of turkey, chicken, salami, juicy pork and beef were forked onto the lower halves of crusty, warm buns. Then the upper halves were dipped in Sam's special homemade sauce and placed on top. Ah, the remembered tang! But she had to wait for Lil. She sat at a small window table and ordered a cup of coffee. At fifteen minutes after eleven, Lil came in.

"Sorry I'm late, my dear. How was your day?"

"Depressing, Aunt Lil. I live so much in the past. I really need to get over my bitterness."

"Oh, I'm sorry, honey."

"It's alright. I'll get past it someday. One of those sandwiches might help. It's been years."

"Well, we can arrange that."

Their lunch was as marvelous as Nora remembered. After eating, they went shopping. As each of them sought a desirable new outfit, Nora marveled at how varied life could be.

# Desairology Class

Much of Nora's cosmetology training carried over from California. Gaining her New York licenses only took two weeks, requiring a mere recertification class taught by Aunt Lil's friend, Bea. Even so, Aunt Lil didn't have an open chair in her shop and her long-time employees had no interest in leaving. Nora took all the fill-in work that became available, but it didn't amount to much. She was still mostly relegated to cleaning up and phone duties for minimal pay. April was passing and Nora's finances were troublesome. She interviewed with a few other salons but had nothing came of it. That was ok, she had scant desire to work elsewhere. Even if most of the shop's customers were of her aunt's generation, Nora wanted to work with and for Lil.

Despite being a low wage, fill-in beautician, Nora was so well taken care of by her aunt and uncle that her life felt more promising than it had in years. Their affections were making deep impressions upon her. She didn't know what she would have done without their constant kindness. Even so, after several weeks of living with them, she was feeling she really should get out on her own. Ideally, she'd work with Lil but live independently. The problem was still money. Unless she found more income she'd never be able to afford an apartment in New York, or even a room.

Lil's desairology class was scheduled to begin behind her salon in early May. Although Nora still had misgivings, something, perhaps the need for rent money, was making her slightly more comfortable with notions of working with the dead. More at ease or not, she still couldn't help wondering why desairologists made corpses presentable when they'd just be stuffed into the ground or burnt up. Sharing tea in Gerry and Lil's living room, she broached her nagging question one evening. "What's the *point*, Auntie? We so rarely treat the living well; why do we care what the dead look like?"

"It's just how we show our respect, honey," Aunt Lil responded. "Other cultures may be different, but…"

"*I'll say* they're different," Gerry roused. "In the Zoroastrian faith, they place corpses atop flat-roofed towers so that vultures, crows and what have you can swoop in and eat them. They consider it to be a last act of charity. *Dakhma,* it's called. Towers of Silence, the English labeled such corpse edifices. If we weren't so squeamish in these parts, I might opt for such an exit myself. Other societies chop their dead into pieces then…"

"Gerry!" Lil cut him off.

"Yes, dear?"

"That is *enough*, thank you!"

"As always, I defer to beauty. I was simply trying to…"

"Simply trying to shock," Aunt Lil cut him off.

"Actually, my dear, I was attempting to indicate how social reactions are very often simply a matter of conditioning."

"You were trying to do both, to shock *and* explain. You don't fool me."

"Ah, caught out again. I should have married a less astute woman. Do you remember Dora Sanders? Why, I could have fooled that one without half trying."

"You fooled me enough that I *married* you."

"Yes," Gerry chuckled, "I did, didn't I? I'm still quite proud of that."

"You should be."

"I am."

"You *should* be."

"I *am.*"

Smiling at their hijinks, Nora rose from the couch. "I'm off to bed."

"Very well, my dear," Gerry said. "Up to your Tower of Silence with you."

"Gerry!" Aunt Lil scolded.

"Good night," Nora said, smiling.

"Good night, dear," her relations responded in unison.

Ascending the stairs, Nora again vowed to keep her eyes fixed upon the future, to give full attention and trust to her coming endeavors. Oftentimes, when doubts crept in, she thought, 'Life's not how it's supposed to be; it's how it *is*. It's how I cope with it that will make all the difference.' Still, the feeling that she had to find a better paying job and make more money kept growing.

Nora's next workday was, like most, exhausting but satisfying. That night after dinner, Lil sat in her recliner next to

Gerry. Putting her feet up, she began speaking of past classes and students. "Do your students ever freak out?" Nora asked.

"I don't know about freaking out," Lil said, "but you never know how people will react. Some get woozy; a few have even fainted. But for others it isn't so creepy. It's always like that; what one person sees as sad or scary, another might find intriguing and another, boring. Some see only a career opportunity. It's best if students have fully considered their feelings about death before enrolling."

"Is that possible?" Gerry chimed in. "*Full* consideration of death?"

"Perhaps not," Lil answered, "but some arrive with more understanding than others. How's that, professor?"

"It'll do, my dear."

"What if *I* freak out?" Nora resumed.

"Oh honey, I doubt that'd happen. But if you did, we'd manage it."

Some days later, Nora's class began. She was one of only four students younger than thirty. The ten others were middle-aged males and females. As if by gravitation, Nora found herself sharing a table with the two other youngest women. When Nora introduced herself, both answered with heavy accents. Lin was a petite Asian and Rana was dark and quite beautiful. Nora wondered where they came from but didn't ask. As Lil made her way to the lectern, the room grew quiet.

"You're here to become desairologists," she began. "Can anyone explain what that means?" Nora knew but, owing to her association with Lil, felt answering would be cheating. When no one else responded, Lil continued, "The term, 'desairology' is derived from combining, 'des' for deceased, 'air' for hair and 'ology', meaning a branch of study. The only other word offered for our art by the Merriam-Webster dictionary is, 'necrocosmetology'.

"Unfortunately, desairology is sometimes disrespected. But here we will honor each other and give the final appearance of the deceased our full regard. A person's funeral is their last bow on life's stage. Desairology's goal is to make the deceased look as good as he or she did in life, or better.

"In addition to your respect, this practice will require patience and effort. It's not always easy, not even for me, even after all these years. The first time I worked on a client who'd passed away, I was quite nervous. Although I was certain I wanted to practice desairology and even anxious to begin, I was nervous. To this day I remember my mentor saying to me, 'This person never hurt you in life, Lil, and she's not going to now.'

"He was right. Not only did my first client not hurt me, she introduced me to a branch of cosmetology that has brought me more fulfillment than I can describe. Practicing what you'll learn here requires maturity, sensitivity and the ability to work efficiently under occasionally very trying circumstances. Victims who've suffered severe trauma, those involved in vehicular accidents or violent crimes, for example, may require extensive procedures in order to make them presentable.

"However, challenging this work can be, when family members tell you how beautiful their mother, sister, wife, father, child, or brother looks, the feeling you get leaves you with a sense of satisfaction that you'll wish everyone could experience at least once. Many of my older customers and I talk about their pending deaths. Together we decide what foundation, nail polish and lipstick they'd like to wear and what hairstyle or color they prefer. I tell you this to explain how intimate your services will sometimes be.

"Along those lines, I want to repeat that I wasn't joking about respect. I will tolerate a little kidding around in this classroom, but only here. If I hear of any levity when you're asked to work on a human being, I will regret having endorsed your certification and will certainly withhold my recommendations.

"Before I begin the demonstration, are there any questions?"

A middle-aged woman raised her hand. When Lil nodded, the lady asked, "Why did I have to be pre-approved for this course?"

"We are not a beauty school," Lil answered. "We don't teach basic cosmetology. We cannot license you as cosmetologists. You have to have those credentials in hand when you apply. We keep a record of our students for certification, endorsements and recertification from Desairology of America. You will receive a one-year membership in D.O.A. upon completing this course. Is there anything else?"

A middle-aged man called out, "How are the job prospects, really?"

"Excellent," Lil answered. "Makeup and hair are usually combined in a funeral home's fee. Your agreements with funeral directors will likely be individual, at least while starting out, so the terms of your work may vary from one establishment to another. This would include the fees for your services and how often you work. It pays considerably better than most earn as a beautician or barber.

"The greatest opportunities in desairology are for nail technicians who also do hair. Only a few funeral homes have on-site cosmetologists, so you'll usually work on an on-call, freelance basis. Desairology is an excellent option for any nail technician who is willing to accept a new challenge. Funeral directors typically have a difficult time finding willing nail technicians, as many are too squeamish to work on the deceased."

"I'm a barber," the man said, "not a nail technician."

"Your certifications are sufficient that you're allowed to take this course," Lil said. "If you want more work, you would be wise to acquire your nail certification. Being a man might give you an advantage. You may be surprised to hear that men often receive more post-mortem care than women. Is there anything else?"

"When I signed up," the same man called, "I assumed we'd be working on corpses here. Now I'm hearing that's not correct."

"You will not be. We will be dealing only with mannequins."

"So, our first actual experience will be our first jobs?" he said. "That doesn't make sense to me."

"Your best course of action would likely be to find a mentor. That's what I did, but it isn't required. Desairologists form a small community, however, and much of your employment will come from word of mouth, so it would be best for you to make and maintain good contacts."

When no additional questions came, Lil said, "We'll start with foundations." She moved toward a mannequin. As she carefully applied foundation to the pale female form, she said, "Remember, you will be the last person to care for this body. Visualize the best possible outcome and strive to make it happen. Give the body as much care and love as you can. Don't let any negative feelings about death show."

She worked quietly for a while. "Now," she said as she finished, "if you will move to a mannequin, two or three students per body, and try to apply foundation as I've shown you... Afterwards, we'll move on to more detailed work."

When they'd each applied foundation, Lil began demonstrating how to deal with nuances. The students took turns attempting to follow Lil's examples. Next, they worked on hands, nails, and necks. Nora and some others seemed tentative. By the time they finished, though, all the mannequins looked at least somewhat improved. Then they covered some basic hairstyling. By the end of the first session Nora was wondering whether any of them would sleep that night.

During the next class, they learned how to dress the corpses. Some laughed in the echoing, tiled space as pairs or trios clothed their male or a female mannequin. But no matter what age or maturity level a student represented, all sobered considerably when working on the faux children. As the days passed, all but a few grew more comfortable and skilled. Some students, however, still succumbed to nervous joking. Nora listened with dismay as some concocted stories regarding whether their dummy had been murdered or mauled, whether they'd succumbed to old age or committed suicide. A few even went so far as to suggest why. But Nora and her new friends, Lin Liang and Rana Jahanfar, took everything quite seriously.

Some students viewed their endeavors as purely tedious, and some continued with their pranks. Lil put up with joking to a point.

She was jovial and friendly as she advised students how to work through various difficulties, but when the pranks went too far, Lil never hesitated to rein them in. As the days passed, Nora grew more comfortable. When she or any other student needed help, Lil would give it. With a few exceptions, Nora felt her fellow students were kind-hearted individuals who intended to give support to mourning families. She made some good friends in that class. But as in most classes, there were also students who didn't thrive.

Rana Jahanfar was a tall, black-haired and energetic 25-year-old Muslim woman. Radiating enthusiasm, she seemed to be always ready for lively conversation. She told Nora that her name meant *beautiful thing* in Farsi but that her Latin American friends teased her by saying that *Rana* meant *frog* in Spanish. Though not pretty, she had a sweet expression and her manners were impeccable. To Nora, Rana seemed an amazing soul.

Lin Liang was a petite, short, striking 24-year-old woman with long, shiny black hair and flashing eyes. She was some type of Christian and always cheerful with whatever came. Seemingly not knowing that mean-spiritedness was even possible, she was one of the finest people Nora had ever met.

Almost immediately, Rana, Lin, and Nora began going to a nearby coffee shop after class. Very soon, Nora thought they were the best friends she'd had since early childhood. Both had qualities that Nora very much admired. Interested in each other's cultures, especially regarding birthdays, weddings and funerals, they rarely ran out of material for conversation.

During their first coffee shop meeting, Rana said, "We do not have desairologist in my country, but we have people who are called *body washers*. In Iran, and many Islamic countries, we must bury our dead within 24 hours. The bodies must be washed before burial. Only women are allowed to wash women and men must wash a man's. We never put makeup on our dead. We don't dress them. We cover the entire body with a piece of white cotton called a *Kafan*. Mourners in Iran must wear only black. Wearing any other color is the ultimate disrespectful thing.

She laughed then continued, "When I was a child everyone said we should avoid the body washers. We were scared of them; they were invariably portrayed as weird and abnormal."

"Well, we *are*, aren't we?" Nora asked.

Smiling, Lin said, "Desairologists in my country are still more widely maligned than almost any other group. They hide their profession from not only their friends and neighbors, but sometimes even their own families. If they know you have that job, they will avoid you and never invite you to parties, weddings, birthdays and family gatherings. Yet those who deal with corpses take care of their loved ones! I think my culture is very cowardly regarding death. I can never let my family or friends know what I am doing. If they find out they will think I am crazy."

Hearing such things, Nora felt almost guilty for how little stigma she'd be subject to. She actually resented how desairology was portrayed in these two other countries. But they didn't just discuss cultural issues. They laughed. They laughed a lot. Walking home alone, reflecting back on the girls who'd most tormented her in high school Nora and Mr. Pino, Nora compared how people could be with how they too often are and nearly wept for the differences.

Although Nora had mainly opted for desairology owing to its job prospects, the possibility of working with Lil and the good pay, feelings of purpose and desires for participation were also growing within her.

As the course completion neared, Lil advised them that working on actual corpses wouldn't be much different than dealing with mannequins, provided they could set aside any fears. But Nora wasn't sure how she'd react, especially if a subject was mangled or, God forbid, a suicide. Lil's advice to her students was constant: "When you're doing makeup on the deceased, regardless of whether they were rich or poor, criminals or victims, never be judgmental. If you rush a job because of some opinion you've formed, I will be ashamed to have taught you.

"Despite what I just said, make sure your immunizations are up to date. Most funeral will have homes you sign a waiver that releases them from liability in the event that you contract something. Keep safe, but give the bodies all the care and love you're capable of, no matter what. Recognize that the person was a son, a daughter, a husband, a father, a mother a grandfather, or grandmother. You must feel responsible for sending them off beautifully."

When the sixth and final session was completed, Lil and her students enjoyed a celebration at the regular coffee shop. Presenting each student with a certificate, Lil showered most with compliments. To a few she was mere, pointedly, no more than polite. Raising her tea in a toast, she said, "I know this wasn't easy for many of you. Whether you found it simple or challenging, I'm proud of you."

Afterwards, Lil asked them what they thought of the experience.

Paul, the only younger male student spoke up, "It might have been the most effective six days of my life. It's weird, desairology teaches us to be desensitized in some ways, but over-sensitizes us in others."

Nora spoke up then, "I'm definitely happy to get my certificate, but there are still things about desairology that worry me. Some I'm not even sure I've even imagined yet. I don't know, maybe I'm just chicken."

"That's an interesting topic for our last night together," Lil said. "How many of you still feel some hesitation?"

Most said that the idea of working on the dead no longer seemed troubling. Nora thought that the few who remained silent were feeling as she did.

"Would you practice desairology on your child, parents, grandparents or siblings?" Lil asked.

Some graduates seemed shocked, but most gave the notion serious thought. Except for Nora and one other student, Patrick, the rest said they would. "I would much rather it be me than some stranger," Lin said. Almost everyone felt the same or similar.

Lil and Nora returned home late. Upon their arrival, Gerry congratulated Nora. Lil patted her cheek and kissed her. It was obvious how proud they were, almost like she was their own daughter. When Gerry asked Nora how she felt about her fears, Nora said, "I'm not totally comfortable with the whole thing yet, Uncle Gerry, but I will be."

# A Still, Silent Room

Nora awoke to a cold, late May morning. After showering and dressing, she went downstairs. Pancakes, sausage, bread, honey and steaming coffee had already been prepared by Lil and Gerry. Despite their continuing hospitality, or because of it, Nora felt she must really cease imposing soon. Today she would have a job interview with Mr. Neal Floyd, the owner and director of Unbridled Spirit Funeral Home, an idea she wasn't very comfortable with.

Lil, who'd secured the interview, also had a morning assignment at Unbridled Spirit: She was to prepare the daughter of one of her long-time salon customers. Josephine Palmer had been only 21 when she passed. The previous night, Lil had pulled out one of her many family albums to show Nora some photos of Josephine. The first picture revealed a 3-year-old girl sitting on her mother's lap in Lil's salon. She'd just had her hair done for the first time. Seeing it distressed Nora so much that she'd refuse to view any more recent photos.

Barely eating, Nora was quietly poking at her eggs when Lil announced, "Well dear, we'd better get moving." As they bundled up in the portico, Gerry began lampooning what he called Nora's "funeral face". Nora had to laugh as she said goodbye to Gerry. At eight, she and Lil stepped out into the cold.

Lil was soon driving through a fine mist. The funeral home was only a couple miles away. The amusement derived from Gerry's hijinks had evaporated off Nora. She had a slight headache and a somewhat worried expression. Nora thought to describe her fears to Lil, but she couldn't quite pinpoint them.

"Honey," Lil said, "you aren't the only person flustered by such passages. I can't say I've never been frustrated by my career. There have been moments of near devastation. Sometimes it seems like too much, but it's always a wonderful education."

Surprised, Nora asked, "Education?"

"One can learn from anything, and more from desairology than from most other... *concerns*. Whoever we are, we all end up with the same fate. And not many really make peace with it. We are a very death-ignoring culture."

Nora smiled. "Maybe the only equality that God's granted us is death!"

Also smiling, Lil agreed, "Yes, we all share at least this one thing. This job may not be easy, but remember… none of us have an *entirely* easy path. Years from now, you may feel quite differently about death. But you'll never know unless you look at it."

"Even if I land this job," Nora said, "with my fear, I'm afraid I'll just quit."

"You'll adjust to desairology sooner than you think. I never felt your fears, Nora. I don't know why that makes me think they're optional, but it does. I was nervous but… I just took things as they came. If I had a bad day, I tried harder and got over it. I just kept telling myself, 'Accept the next challenge.' It all turned out OK. You'll be fine."

Nora wasn't so certain. She was unhappy. Something felt missing. She remembered how, during childhood, she and her cousins could hardly wait to visit Lil's house or salon, where they'd almost certainly encounter new and interesting things. *That* was happiness, not poking over corpses. Shockingly, her own mind suddenly snapped at her, 'Oh, *grow up* already!'

"We're here, honey," Nora said, turning the car into a medium-sized, tree-shrouded parking lot. Past trees' budding branches, Unbridled Spirit Funeral Home seemed to fill the entire grey sky. The immense, two-story, off-white Victorian house seemed nearly daunting. Nora could only stare at it as Lil parked, lost between fear and curiosity. Nora stepped from Lil's Ford. Lil took Nora's elbow and they were moving, passing hedges and the still somewhat winter brown lawn.

They were ascending front steps, five or so. Gaining the gigantic front porch, Lil stopped. Taking Nora's shoulders in both hands, she turned her niece to face her then said, "I told Neal to bring you to the make-up room after your interview. I'd like you to assist me."

"Oh God," Nora mumbled.

"Don't let fear stop you! *Face* this. Just see it more clearly. Does that make sense, honey?"

Nora forced a smile. "I understand what you're saying Aunt Lil, but I can't help it."

"You can. I'll help you help it. Everyone in this building is a friend. They'll help too."

"OK."

They parted immense doors and then entered spacious lobby. A slender woman, 50-ish with a long, gaunt face, was rising from behind an immense reception desk. "Hello, Lil!" the homely woman beamed. She wore a black blouse, tight black skirt, no lipstick and her teeth were immense. Nora thought she looked like a famished mule. "Good morning!" the lady called while approaching. "How are you today?"

"Fine, thank you, Evelyn. And you?"

"Also fine. So, this would be your beautiful niece?"

"Yes, this is Nora."

"Nice to meet you, Nora"

"Likewise," she said

Nora and Evelyn shook hands.

"Mr. Floyd is expecting you," Evelyn said. "Please, go right up."

"Thank you," Lil said.

Leading Nora down a long hall, Lil explained each door they passed. "This is the service hall," she said, gesturing through wide double doors into a cavernous room. Briefly, Nora glimpsed an organ, rows of dark brown chairs and towering stained-glass windows. Continuing on, Lil said, "This leads to the refrigeration room, a makeup room, an embalming room and cremation facilities."

As they began ascending an ornate, curving stairway, Lil went on, "There are offices and an employee lounge upstairs but not much else." An aroma of coffee wafted through the second-story hallway. The first office door was open. Halting outside it, Lil called, "Hello, Neal, may we come in?"

The suit-clad man greeted them brightly, "Of course, Lil. Good morning."

As they entered, Mr. Floyd stood from behind his cluttered desk. Neal was a tall, handsome man, with broad shoulders and lots of white hair. He looked to be in his middle sixties. His white shirt, black tie, and black suit were perfectly pressed.

Lil hugged Mr. Floyd before introducing Nora. Mr. Floyd gave her a warm handshake. "How nice to meet you, dear."

"Thank you," Nora replied. "Nice to meet you, sir. How are you?"

"Very well, thanks. I've heard a lot of good things about you."

"Thank you. My aunt is, um... nice."

Nora thought Neil very good looking for his age. From her aunt and uncle, she had heard quite a bit about how beloved he was to the community. He was the owner of the Unbridled Spirit funeral home, single, never been married. Returning behind his desk, he motioned toward two chairs. As the women sat, he said, "Can I get you anything, coffee or tea?"

"Please," Lil answered, "coffee would be very nice."

Somewhat uncomfortable, Nora declined.

Neal left. A minute later, he came back in carrying Lil's steaming cup. He sat behind his desk. As Mr. Floyd and Aunt Lil sipped coffee and chatted, Nora noted that the office held not a single photograph or painting, only the framed words of Emily Dickinson which hung on the wall behind his desk, "If I can stop one heart from breaking, I shall not live in vain; if I can ease one life the aching, or cool one pain, or help one fainting robin, unto his nest again, I shall not live in vain."

Eventually, Mr. Floyd opened a desk drawer. He took out two sheets of paper and a black pen. Sliding them toward Nora he said, "Here's an application, Nora. Also, I need to make copies of your cosmetology, desairlogy, nail and driver's licenses."

Nora handed over her materials. He left to copy them. Nora was still filling out the application when Neal returned with her documents. She continued working while Lil and Neal began discussing Josephine. The poor girl had died from Lou Gehrig's disease. Lil and Neal lamented that, in this age of miraculous medical advances, there was still so little treatment for neurodegenerative illnesses.

"I think about Josephine all the time," Lil said. "It was devastating for me when she was diagnosed. Imagine how her family feels."

"There's nothing worse than losing a child," Neal said. "It's just not the right order of things. I guess sometimes *right* doesn't figure in."

Struggling to focus, Nora wasn't enjoying listening about Josephine. As they continued conversing, Nora wondered, 'How can these people start their day with such sorrow? How can they bear the sadness and still handle their everyday lives?'

After a while, Lil asked Neal, "Is she ready for makeup?"

"Yes. She's dressed and ready. I'll call George now, let him know you're coming down."

Rising, Lil said, "I can't tell you how difficult this preparation will be for me."

"I know. It's very trying, preparing someone you loved. But Josephine would be glad it's you. We'll join you shortly."

"OK," Lil said, "see you down there." She was gone.

Neal phoned George. "Has Josephine been transferred to makeup?"

George must've answered in the negative.

"Please do so. Lil's on her way. Thanks."

When Neal hung up, Nora handed him the completed application.

"Thank you, Nora. Considering all your aunt has told me, I'm sure this is just a formality."

"Mr. Floyd, can I ask you something?"

"Sure, Nora. And please, call me Neal."

"It's little embarrassing to ask this but, how can you deal with so much pain and suffering? Don't you ever wonder about mortality?"

Neal thought for a moment. Then smiling, he said, "I do but… It's still a mystery. You just show up and get to it, I guess. It used to rattle me a bit. It still does, but differently. Appropriately, I guess. We think we can deceive things in life, but nothing fools death. It's absolutely certain. We can question everything in life, but not death; it's the only thing in life that's certain." He paused then, "I don't know if that helped. Anything else?"

"No. And thank you. Everything seems to help a little. Every sincere word I've heard these last few months have each helped a little bit."

"Well, that's a nice sentiment. Now, I have a few questions for you."

Nora smiled. "Of course."

"The majority of cosmetologists have no interest in becoming desairologists. Why do you want to work here?"

"In all honesty, I didn't want to. I just need a job." She paused and then added, "I hope I don't ruin this, but I never even thought of desairology before moving to New York. But when my aunt offered this path… I love her so much that I couldn't refuse. When Aunt Lil brought it up, this tiny voice started calling me, insisting. Everyone wants a great job in a happy, pleasant environment, right? But with my present life's situation, it seems impossible for now. I need a decent job. If Aunt Lil thinks desairology is the best thing for me, I believe her."

"I like your honesty," Mr. Floyd said. "So many set out intending some kind of amazing life and then wind up on journeys that are entirely different from what we planned. But sometimes it's necessary to do something else to earn a living. When I was young, I'd wanted to be a farmer or own a nursery. Plants were my passion. Instead, rather than studying life and growth, I wound up witnessing death every day. In the beginning it was devastating, but I've adjusted. Everyone who knew me before would be very surprised to find me in the funeral business. But that's what happened."

"How come?" Nora asked.

"Really? You want to hear this?"

"Yes."

"Well, it's pretty simple. This was my parents' business. As much as I wanted to pursue my own interests… When I was twenty, my father passed away. Not long after, my mother became sick. I asked her to sell, but she wouldn't. So I left college and took over. In the beginning, it was painful, but… if you really feel that you're helping people, it goes a long way towards displacing youthful imaginings. Death can be a very burdensome reality. But I soon realized that I had a gift for helping people deal with it. That gave me strength. People come here for comfort. If you can give it, they'll remember you fondly forever. Or for however long forever lasts."

Mr. Floyd struck Nora as intelligent and good-natured. And she found his words interesting.

"But did you ever feel happy in this work?" Nora asked.

"Eventually, yes. In the beginning, no. But after I'd occupied this position for a few months, my opinion changed. I've worked in this funeral home for forty years now," he continued. "Generally, it's not an easy or popular job. God knows how many eyes I've closed over the years. I've comforted thousands. It's a sad business, but it can somehow make you feel alive and contented. From what you've said, this isn't ideal, not the kind of employment that will make your soul sing. But if you stick with it, you may soon find that you're making real differences in people's lives. The end of your days will often be better than their beginnings. To me, that's a pretty big deal."

Neal was quiet for some seconds, then, "So, Nora, you and I are quite alike. Neither of us wanted to work in this field. But my advice to you is, accept the first and the best opportunity you can find to earn your living, but continue to prepare the way for your leading aims. Now, so if I offer you the job, will you accept?"

Somewhat surprised, Nora heard herself say, "Yes. I'd be very grateful, Mr. Floyd.

"Then the job's yours. We'll try you out as an independent contractor, providing services as-needed. I'll pay you $30 an hour." Nora was stupefied. Almost unbelievably, she'd never asked what she might be earning. She'd assumed she'd be making more than she had as a mid-level beautician, but $30 an hour seemed like a fortune.

"Like many funeral homes," Neal was saying, "we don't have an in-house desairologist. Lil's our usual go-to gal. Some homes hire embalmers who also provide desairologist services. I've been thinking of going that route for some time now. If things work out, and you get an embalming certificate, I'll consider hiring you full time with a salary and benefits."

"Thank you, Mr.… Neal. Thank you so much for the opportunity."

"You're welcome.

"Shall we go see what Lil's up to?"

"I'm still nervous, but yes."

He led her out. On their way downstairs they ran into a bald, very chubby, short fellow. Whistling as he climbed toward them, he seemed quite cheerful. "Good morning, Neal" the man hailed up.

"Hello, George," Neal responded. "Nora, this is George, our only full time driver. George, meet Nora, our newest on-call desairologist."

"Very pleased to meet you, young lady."

"Likewise," Nora said.

Continuing past them, George said, "Make yourself at home here."

To Nora, it seemed an odd thing to say. But there was no time to ponder it. Neal had already resumed his descent. Downstairs, as they continued down the hall and Neal explained the various processes that transpired from the moment of a body's arrival, a feeling of awe and dread came over Nora. As they passed more open doors, Nora peeked in.

A woman of about seventy and a man about forty sat in one room. The woman was crying, dabbing her eyes with Kleenex. Her lap was filled with folded clothing. In the next room, a family of seven or eight was crowded around a conference table, whispering. Rounding a corner at the end of the hall, a sealed door appeared. It's four-inch, dark blue letters read, MAKEUP. Beneath it another sign written in red said, AUTHORIZED PERSONEL ONLY.

Neal knocked but immediately opened the door. Nora followed him in. Lil, wearing a white overcoat and gloves, was sitting in a black office chair next to a beautiful white casket. She smiled at them, but sadly. Each side of the pale coffin was splendidly engraved with red-beaked black swans. "How's it going?" Neal asked Lil.

"Fine. Considering."

"OK. Well, here's your niece. I've got a nine o'clock meeting."

"See you later," Lil answered.

Neal was leaving, closing the door.

Nora's eyes roved the room but avoided the coffin. Four tremendous double-hung windows allowed light to flood in. White, bare walls reflected morning sunlight. It was cold and smelled of hairspray. In the far-right corner were two small rolling tables. Atop each were foundations, assorted lipsticks, nail polishes, brushes, combs, hairspray, bottles of alcohol, cotton swabs and boxes of stretch vinyl gloves. Two black office chairs like the one Lil sat in were by the left wall. Next to the chairs was a metal clothing rack holding a few white frocks and Lil's navy-blue jacket.

"Honey," Lil was saying, "put on one of those frocks then grab a chair and come help me."

Less than five feet from the coffin, Nora finally looked to its contents. Only the lower half of Josepine's body was visible. Even so, it terrified her. She knew it was irrational but didn't dare go closer. Her spirits sank. She was considering leaving.

"Honey?" Aunt Lil was saying. "Did you hear me? You can't work without a frock, dear."

Nora didn't answer but somehow started moving. Passing the casket, she wouldn't look into it. She removed a cleaned, pressed uniform from the hanger. Slowly, she slid into it. Barely moving, she closed each button. She then began rolling a chair toward the casket. A few feet behind Lil, she stopped then just stood there, clasping the rolling seat. The casket, the smell of hairspray and what little she could see of Josephine were all making it hard to think.

To buy time, she said, "Do you mind if I close some shutters, Aunt Lil?"

"Well, the light can only help us dear, but… go ahead."

When Nora had spent a full minute slowly sealing out the brightness, Lil turned to her. "Come here already, Nora! I want you to work on her hands."

Nora tried to say no. She looked to the floor. Her heart was beating like a jackhammer. In a subdued tone she said, "I don't think I can do this, Aunt Lil. I'm so sorry."

There was a brief silence. Looking disappointed, Lil rose and went to Nora. Putting an arm around her niece, she asked, "What's wrong, dear?"

"I know it's childish, but I can't do it. I'm completely terrified."

Nora was hoping Lil would tell her to wait outside, but her aunt looked at her with an ironic gleam in her eyes. Sounding slightly chastising, she said, "Good heavens, Nora, if you think something is impossible, it will be. I know you're afraid, and that's fine, but the sooner you face this the sooner you'll overcome it."

Nora thought Lil didn't understand. Josephine was her age, for God's sake!

Lil took her arm then said, "Come on, there's nothing to be afraid of."

They moved closer. Motioning, Lil said, "Look at her, the poor dear. There's nothing scary about her. She's sleeping."

Josephine's round face was beautiful. Her chin was dimpled and her hair long, brown and lustrous. But she was utterly motionless. Her dress was beaded, white Chantilly lace. Concentrating on courage, Nora stared blankly. After a moment, she whispered, "She's beautiful."

Lil nodded. "She can't hear you, honey. Even if she could, why would you whisper such a thing?"

As if she hadn't heard Lil, Nora exclaimed, "She was so young! Life isn't fair!"

"I know, honey. But what can we do?" Lil took Nora's chair and then pulled it alongside the casket. Nora sat. Lil rolled one of the small, laden tables to Nora then returned to her own seat. Sitting opposite her niece, she said, "Please remove Josephine's old nail polish and then apply the pink. When you've finished with that hand, we'll switch sides so you can work over here."

Nora said, "I don't dare touch her. I'm scared."

"There's nothing to scare you," said Lil. "She's dead."

Her aunt's calmness amazed Nora.

"Just relax," Lil said. "Focus on your job. If you're really too uncomfortable, wait outside. I'll finish myself."

Embarrassed, Nora grimaced. "Auntie Lil, can I ask you something?"

"Of course."

"How can you repeatedly bear such images? Where do you find the strength?"

"It really isn't strength for me, honey. I'm not overcoming any fear. Quite the opposite, I feel that helping Josephine helps me, perhaps more than her."

"How can a fearful person like me feel that way?"

"Oh honey, just stick to a difficult job until it's done. Keep doing it, bearing more, seeing more. Like everything else in life, you'll adapt."

Nora found the words interesting, but they didn't make sense to her.

"All right," Nora said, "Maybe that's what I'll have to do. The trouble is, I'm afraid of touching her."

Showing real frustration for the first time, Lil snapped, "Would you like to leave, Nora?"

Nora thought for nearly a minute before saying, "No."

"Then quit stressing us both out! Focus on your job!"

Shamed, Nora nodded but initiated nothing. After a few silent minutes, Lil asked, "How did the interview go?"

"Good. Mr.… Neal… he offered me on-call work. I'm so glad he isn't watching right now."

"Well, he soon will be, honey. You'd best get busy."

"I really like him. I'd like to work for him."

"That's excellent, dear. I like him too."

Watching Lil apply facial touchups, Nora's panic subsided a bit. Even so, she just sat there, gazing at Josephine's long, slim fingers. She took a few deep breaths. Actually trembling, she took Josephine's delicate hand in her own. Josephine was cold as ice. Her skin felt like fine porcelain. As Nora began removing the chipped red polish, the negative thoughts whizzing through her compounded her shame. She found her task repulsive, but continued. After softening the chipped edge of Josephine's nails with a file, Nora opened the bottle of pink.

Although Nora felt chilled, beads of sweat were forming on her forehead. The sweat in her eyebrows dripped over her lids. She wiped it away with the back of her wrist. She felt unable to focus on applying the polish. 'What am I doing here?' she wondered. 'This is unbearable.' Not since her father's death had Nora felt so rattled.

All was quiet. Every few minutes, Nora would look to Lil. She stared in horror as Lil brushed the young woman's hair, softly and to the right. Watching, Nora thought, 'How can my aunt be so calm? How has she been doing this for so many years?'

Returning her attention to Josephine's hand, Nora realized that she'd messed up two fingers. Blushing far more than was called for, she apologized. "Sorry, Aunt Lil, I messed up. I'll do better."

Lil looked at the work in question. "It is not perfect, honey, but it's OK. I've seen much worse. Do it again if you like. If not, we're fine."

Nora cleaned away her flawed work and then began again. Soon, they were switching seats. Nora managed Josephine's other hand pretty well. Lil watched as Nora carefully applied polish. Nora felt relief when Lil smiled and said, "Well done, Nora!"

Finished with Josephine's hands, Nora asked, "Is there anything else you want me to do?"

"No, honey. I'm almost done. You try and relax."

Nora took off her uniform and then dropped it in the rolling rack's hamper. She went to the bathroom and washed. Back in the makeup room, she gazed through one of the tall windows. The mist had lifted. It was beautiful out: the sun looked down from quiet skies. Staring blankly, she marveled at what she'd just done.

Lil was stroking the last bit of mascara on Josephine's eyelashes. "She's ready. I'll let Neal know." She rolled her chair to a nearby wall phone. Within seconds she was informing Neal that Josephine was ready for the service room. Nora wished that she didn't have to go to Josephine's service or attend her burial, but her aunt had previously made it clear that she had to.

Lil hung up and then surprised Nora by saying, "We've got a few minutes, hon. Would you like to get some coffee before the viewing?"

# Josephine

Nora and Lil entered the small employees lounge. No one was there. As Lil made coffee, Nora took a seat at a round, plastic table.

"What do you think of Neal?" Lil asked.

"Too much to describe," she said. "He can't be as good as my first impression says. I'd rather see him a second time before giving an opinion."

"Very well, Nora, but when you've seen him a second time, you'll think twice as much of him, and it will take twice as long to tell me about it. Every time you meet him, he'll seem twice as wonderful."

Smiling, Nora changed the subject, "I can't believe how slowly time passed in there, Aunt Lil. It felt like days."

"This may sound harsh, dear, but that's entirely owing to your self indulgence. Sometimes I think you love your fears more than your want to be rid of them."

As Nora doubtfully digested Lil's words, George entered along with a small, broad-shouldered, middle-aged man. "Nora," George said, "this is our primary embalmer, Amos Pesta. Amos, Nora. Looks like she'll be working with us."

Thinking that Amos looked more like a bank manager than some ghoulish embalmer, Nora said, "Nice to meet you, Amos."

"Pleased to meet you too, Nora. I look forward to working with you."

"Coffee will be ready in a minute," Lil said.

The men sat with Nora.

"Any pickups scheduled today?" Lil asked George.

"Yeah," he answered, "A weird one. You may've read about this guy; died from a heart attack a couple days back, wore tattered clothes and lived in the projects; turns out he was rich as Croesus, left behind a few million!"

"Oh my gosh!" Lil exclaimed.

"Can you believe it?" George continued. "This guy clipped coupons but left millions to like, six or seven charities and nothing for his family. They had no idea what he was worth. I mean, they knew he had some investments but… They just thought he was stingy. He never let on. Can you imagine?"

Shaking his dignified head, Amos said, "They must be pretty shocked. And hurt."

"Maybe," Nora put in, "he thought all that money was necessary for his survival, but that spending it wouldn't brighten his life."

"What?!" George exclaimed. "Where'd that come from? Why posit anything? Maybe he just felt good about hiding things. Maybe he was just plain loony."

"Or maybe," Lil said, "he simply didn't want to be badgered. We'll never know why some people do what they do. Years ago, a customer of mine had a millionaire friend. When this woman died, she'd left everything to her cat, Chitter-Chatter. I swear it was like something from a cartoon."

"How long ago, Aunt Lil?" Nora asked. "Is Chitter-Chatter still alive?"

"Oh yes. The cat's still ticking. She must be almost fifteen by now. She has her own staff and owns a mansion."

"What happens when she dies?"

"Everything will be donated to the ASPCA."

"Did this lady have kids?" Amos asked.

"Yes, but she didn't leave them a thing, not a cent!"

"Ouch!" Amos blurted. "The guy on my table now didn't have to fake poverty. His was the real deal. You should see all he's done to himself, the damage to his circulatory system! And the stink off this guy! In all my years here, I don't think I've come across a riper specimen!"

Noticing Nora's suddenly peaked expression, Lil said, "Amos, perhaps we could discuss something else?"

"What? Since when do you…?" Then, glancing at Nora, he seemed to get it. "Sure. Sorry. You guys catch the Jets game last night?"

Smiling into his steaming cup, George said, "That's our most gruesome topic yet."

Ignoring George, Amos rose. "Well, I'd better get going. Duty calls."

"Yeah," George concurred, "I should get back too."

Amos was extending his hand to Nora. "See you soon, kid."

Taking his clean, warm hand in hers, imagining all it'd been through, she felt like she was befriending a monster. Smiling while trying to limit imaginings, she said, "I've been asking everyone how they deal with this work, Amos. How do you cope?"

Releasing her hand, Amos thought for a second. "I don't know. If someone had told me fifteen years ago that I'd be an embalmer, I'd have told them they were nuts. But sometimes life takes unexpected turns. Consider Chitter-Chatter, eating caviar, ordering imported mice and whatever. Anyway, I guess most of us become creatures of habit, doing the same thing over and over."

Laughing, George jumped in, "Same with me, kid. When I first started here, I couldn't stand it. But stand it I did, and for years now."

"You have to be strong to deal with death all the time," Amos continued.

"What?!" George blurted. "What're you talking about? We're strong?"

"I guess what I mean is," Amos shifted, "you have to be somewhat free from fear of it, at least in others, maybe in yourself, too, to some degree. I don't know. Death doesn't mean that much to me. I doubt it means what a lot of people think it does. It doesn't bother me, though. I do my job and sleep OK."

As Nora retreated within herself, Amos said, "'Bye Lil. Nora, I look forward to working with you."

Now rising also, George said, "Yeah. See you two."

When the two men were gone, Lil said, "Well, Nora, are you ready for Josephine's viewing?"

Not ready at all, Nora said, "Sure."

They went into the hall and toward the service room. Neal stood before the vast chamber's wide doors with a tall, heavyset, bespectacled priest. The two men were greeting arriving mourners. Nora and Lil kept back for a few minutes. When a gap opened up, Lil took Nora's elbow and guided her forward.

"Hello ladies," Neal greeted them. "Nora, this is Father Joseph. Father Joseph, meet our newest desairlologist, Nora."

"Pleased to meet you, Nora," the giant priest rumbled.

"Likewise."

Additional mourners were arriving, so Lil and Nora entered the service chamber. Silently, they took seats in one of the rear rows. The room remained quiet. Nora felt that she had entered a quietude as deep as the fathomless sea. The room was all hardwood floors, polished mahogany and angel-depicting tapestries. The ceiling was adorned with a dozen or so inlaid star-shaped lights. "The first two rows," Lil's voice cut into Nora's foggy anxiety, "are usually family and close friends."

Nora nodded. A few chairs to Nora's left, a thin, short young woman of about her own age was sobbing. Except for her silver angel earrings, she was entirely clad in black. Some people were covering their noses and mouths with handkerchiefs. Others were just gloomily quiet. There were about sixty mourners. Perhaps a third were weeping.

Lost amidst the dreary black attire, soft classical music and grief, Nora felt very tired. Her back was hurting. Listening to the steady sobs of Josephine's mother, grandmothers, aunts, and uncles, Nora wished she wasn't there. She wasn't expecting to feel so restless. She couldn't bear to see anyone suffer.

Gazing about, she thought, 'Every wall, every chair, every curtain here sweats with torment.' Nora thought of Neal's words from only hours before, "You can question everything in life, but not death; the only certain thing in life is death."

Such recollections didn't help. She tried not to think about anything. Uncalled for visions of her dad's suicide and funeral flooded her: the yard and its tree and the funeral. She made another effort at diverting her thoughts. She listened to her heartbeat and breathing. She wanted to get up and go home. Nora closed her eyes. Her face blank, her mind kept racing across scenes from her childhood. When it seemed that everyone had arrived, the priest and Neil came in.

Lil placed her hand on Nora's wrist and then leaned against her. Nora's eyes filled with tears. Lil put her arm around her niece then pulled her close. Josephine's parents, grandparents and relatives, all in the front row, were crying. Nora thought Josephine's mother and grandmothers would never stop. Finally, Father Joseph started conducting the service. Mourner's sighs and sobs quieted down as the large priest began speaking:

"O MERCIFUL GOD, the Father of our LORD JESUS CHRIST, who is the resurrection and the life; in whom whosoever believeth, shall live, though he die; and whosoever liveth, and believeth in him, shall not die eternally; who also hath taught us, by his holy Apostle Saint Paul, not to be sorry, as men without hope, for those who sleep in him; We humbly beseech thee, O FATHER, to raise us from the death of sin unto the life of righteousness; that, when we shall depart this life, we may rest in him; and that, at the general Resurrection in the last day, we may be found acceptable in thy sight; and receive that blessing, which thy well-beloved Son shall then pronounce to all who love and fear thee, saying, Come, ye blessed children of my Father, receive the kingdom prepared for you from the beginning of the world. Grant this, we beseech thee, O merciful FATHER, through JESUS CHRIST, our Mediator and Redeemer. Amen."

As the priest went on, Nora was surprised to find that she found the words beautiful. When Father Joseph finished, a few family members and friends rose and went forward. One by one, they spoke of Josephine's short life. Josephine's mother, a tall, pale woman in her mid-forties went forward to speak. She stood looking

122

over the gathering, looking lost. Quite beautiful, she was perhaps five-nine and adorned in a plain black dress. She couldn't talk. Her eyes were swollen and bloodshot. Swallowing tears, she returned to her seat. Other loved ones arose and spoke.

One of Josephine's grandfathers, a frail looking man wearing a black hat and bowtie beneath an old beige coat, was sleeping. An ornately carved, dark wooden cane rested across his lap. Seeing Nora staring at him, Lil whispered, "He's been a bit lost for some while now, honey." Nora thought they must be out of their minds to bring him there.

Josephine's loved ones continued describing the girl's short life. To Nora it seemed surreal that, in the face of their despair, they'd address a crowd. As people described their memories, it seemed like the mourners were on an emotional roller coaster, up one minute and down the next. 'This can't be healthy,' Nora thought. 'I don't like it. People are insane. All cultures are insane.' She thought of Gerry's Tower of Silence, and somewhat understood the old loon's preference.

Father Joseph was again at the lectern. Following his closing prayers, the viewing began. Neil positioned himself beside the casket. Josephine's parents and immediate family were up, taking their time. Her mother kissed her daughter, "We love you. We miss you…" Then she burst into tears. Her whole body was shaking. Her husband put his arms around her. Whispering something, he half carried her away. They'd gone only a few steps when she turned and sort stumbled back. Looking down at Josephine, she burst into hysterics. As her husband and others tried to guide her away, she took Josephine's hand, drew it to her lips and kissed it before gently laying it down again.

Watching, Nora thought, 'This has to be the most painful moment of that woman's life! This is what I'll be doing for a living? Watching these scenes again and again?!'

As Josephine's mother passed Nora, others approached the casket. One by one, mourners left, some walking arm in arm. When almost everyone had left, Nora and Lil went forward. They looked at their work for some seconds and then turned for the doors.

With lumps in their throats and tears in their eyes, Lil and Nora offered Jospehine's parents their condolences. "I join you in your grief," Lil said. Both parents were hugging Lil, telling her how beautiful her daughter looked. Nora, not knowing what to say, stood by silently. She tried to feel calm, but there was a raw burning inside her. She started crying.

Lil told the parents that Nora had assisted with Josephine's makeup. Her mother looked at Nora then hugged her. In a wispy voice, she said, "Thank you for making our angel beautiful." And then she began weeping again, but softly. Josephine's father, his weary eyes swollen with tears, said, "She looks just perfect. Thank you."

Nora couldn't speak. Her thoughts were as cloudy as her eyes. Lil was speaking to Jospehine's parents. Nora couldn't comprehend. She was leading Nora away. How on earth would she be able to endure this each and every week?! It simply wouldn't be possible. Her emotions would drown her!

When everyone had left for the cemetery, Nora and Lil stepped out onto the stone entryway. Nora looked to the sun's orange orb and listened to the winds' soughing nearly noiselessly through the trees' budding branches. Looking to the traffic and bustling crowds, it seemed almost impossible that the world could be hurrying along so unmindful of what she'd just seen. It looked so unconcerned. And even those who'd been at the viewing would soon be carrying on with their busy lives, their families, careers, friends

and other blessings. How was it possible?

# Post Josephine

After Nora and Lil left the funeral home, they stopped for lunch at Lil's regular deli. When they'd ordered and settled at a table Lil leaned in and asked Nora "Do you think you'd be comfortable doing a job on your own?"

Nora couldn't believe Lil was asking such a thing. Hadn't she just watched her niece nearly lose it? Following a brief silence, Nora answered, "I don't know, Aunt Lil. I'm happy it's over. It was pretty unnerving."

"How so, dear?"

"Seeing the families, their broken hearts, their despair. Aunt Lil, how have you dealt with watching so much suffering for so long?"

"Look, Nora, you make far too much of this. If you'd just buck up and face the fact that my job is a service and not a horror show, you'd have no difficulty seeing it as I do."

Again rebuffed by her loving aunt, Nora wasn't sure whether she was going to pursue the job. "I'm fooling myself and wasting everyone's time. I'll never be a well-adjusted desairologist. It's too much for me."

"Probably not," Aunt Lil responded coldly. "Nobody's *cut out* for desairology. We are who we choose to be. If your choices align with your abilities, you'll achieve success. I know some aspects can be burdensome, but if you're like me, and I suspect you may be, you may someday find that indispensable duties make you content."

"I don't know, Aunt Lil."

"Don't give up yet, honey! Time and effort will resolve your qualms, perhaps not immediately, but eventually."

Nora sank deeper into Lil's contentions and her own misgivings. "How can that be, Aunt Lil?"

Lil thought for a moment. "You must change, dear. Transformation is almost always emotional. The question here is: Do you want to wallow in your phobias or overcome them? You may have to sail over waves of emotions concerning death and sorrow. Will you roll with those waves and outlast them, or will you let the storm defeat you?

"Believe me, this job may help you become properly compassionate regarding death and yet somewhat desensitized to its harsher elements. Daunting tasks may soon become habitual. You'll see yourself, others, and life in new ways. Believe it or not, if you outlast this storm, you'll wind up celebrating life more, not less. Serenity will replace anxiety. If you continue assisting people through painful times, helping their lives run more smoothly, it will bring you pleasure and purpose."

Lil became silent. Nora didn't know what to say.

"For me," Lil continued, "this job confirms my faith. I can't imagine doing anything without surrendering to God's will. Put your trust in God, dear. When it comes to death, we must resign to what will be. The more you practice giving your burdens to God, the more exciting everything becomes. Seeing how He handles the things we can't do anything about is amazing! People rarely become comfortable with death. It's messy. It seems to have no rules or boundaries. But it does."

Their sandwiches were arriving, brought by a smiling young waitress. "Can I get you anything else?" she asked.

"No thank you," Lil smiled. "We're all set."

As the young woman left, Lil resumed her counsel, "If death is a dark place of endless night, then grief and loss form a black, bottomless pit. But my faith suggests that death isn't what many imagine it to be. All mourners wish that their beloved ones weren't taken from them, but we all leave each other, at least for a time. Rather than run from it, accept the suffering. Study it. We must channel our emotions as properly as God allows. We must trust God. He brings welcome beauty and unequalled comfort."

Nora wasn't certain. Comprehending God's wishes, or pretending to, and finding trust in Him simply weren't part of her background.

Seeing Nora's ongoing struggle, Lil continued, "Give yourself time, Nora. You may try and succeed or try and fail. Either way, it's better to try than not. Just stick with it. These emotions may subside and then everything will become habitual, but not in a bad way. Fear is a habit. This job has taught me as much about life and success as anything else I've ever done. Each service teaches something. This job, just like climbing mountains, strengthens you. You tap reserves you never knew you had. Doubt evaporates. Know who you are and what you can do. Lesson number one: Persevere. Lesson number two: Find your calm in the face of suffering. It's there if you look."

Leaning over, Lil pulled Nora close and kissed her cheek. "I understand your hesitations, honey. When I started this job I felt somewhat similar. Less so, but... I can't tell you how happy I am that I took it up."

Gazing at her capable aunt, Nora felt like a seven-year-old girl again.

"When I was young," Aunt Lil went on, "I wanted to go into theater, to become an actress. I never imagined I'd wind up working in funeral homes."

"Everyone's been telling me that, Aunt Lil. You, George, Art, Mr. Floyd..."

"Then maybe you should listen, dear. In any case I don't regret having conceded my dreams for this. I have a small business that helps people. I really can't imagine asking for more. The more you assist others, the greater your sense of personal power becomes."

Nora's tense smile barely screened her thought, 'Easier said than done.'

Lil then shifted, "Would you really like to quit, dear? Maybe I've been pressuring you too much. We wouldn't hold it against you. Many find they aren't cut out for this. I'd like you to continue. I think it'd be good for you, but there's no shame in stopping. You could simply practice cosmetology."

Recollecting Mr. Floyd's lucrative offer, Nora wondered, 'Is that why I'd continue? Just for the money?' "I don't know, Aunt Lil. One minute I'm sure I'll quit, and then the next I think I should stick with it. I'm still doubtful. I couldn't feel the reality of death in your classes, but today I did. I guess I'm in shock."

"Focus more on your strengths than your hesitation, honey."

"I'll try," Nora said uncertainly.

"I'm sure you can adapt," said Lil with certainty. "It's less a question of if you *can* than if you *will*. We should probably eat these sandwiches, don't you think?"

Smiling, Nora nodded. Eating, watching people coming and going, Nora felt on the edge of a new world, one she might either settle in or topple from. Trying to keep her negative emotions in check, she thought, 'What I don't understand far exceeds what I do. Is it my awareness of this is that makes me human?'

They finished their sandwiches then left. As they were going out, a young woman carrying a baby was entering. Holding the door open for her, looking at her child, Nora thought, 'What is the point of being born at all?'

Outside, a cold, biting wind had come up. Amazed by the day's rapid shifts from gloomy to sunny to blustery, Nora gazed up at scudding clouds. When the women arrived home, Nora was psychologically worn out. She felt as if she'd come from hard labor. Even so, she showered and changed and then set out for Lil's salon. She worked until five. Lil stayed home to cook and do paperwork.

As the last customer left, Nora closed up. She swept the floors and tidied the place. When she returned to Gerry and Lil's, her uncle greeted her with a warm hug and kiss. "How was your first day at the funeral home, Nora?"

"Unbelievable, Uncle Gerry."

"Huh. That's evasive. Good or bad?"

A bit sadly she said, "Well, not that bad for the first experience, I guess. But I have a lot to think about. I'll probably stare at the walls all night."

"Heck, everyone needs a little wall staring now and then."

"I guess."

"Just remember, Nora, these are just emotional troubles. Everyone get them."

"Must every day be a struggle, Uncle Gerry?"

"Can you really say that each and every day is nothing but struggle, Nora? I've got nothing against occasional self-pity… Heck, I even indulge in a bit myself."

"It's all too much."

"It isn't, Nora. A life without suffering may sound great, but we can't escape its complexities. Weary, we entice ourselves with dreams of unreality, then grow increasingly uncomfortable. Your troubles are like soda bubbles; they rise to the surface and pop."

"Thank you," Nora said, half meaning it.

Aunt Lil came in. "Dinner will be ready soon," she said. "Do you want to go freshen up, Nora?"

"Sure," she said.

Nora went upstairs to wash. She then sat by the window and simply stared out. Less than half an hour later, Lil was calling her to dinner. Lil had prepared another feast: fried chicken, mashed potatoes, green beans and biscuits. Nora watched Lil and Gerry enjoying their dinner as usual. For the first time since her arrival, she felt somewhat alienated. After eating, Nora did the dishes.

Before long, they were all sitting by the fireplace, enjoying homemade walnut cake. Lil was telling Gerry about Josephine's funeral. Uncertain why, Nora could barely stand hearing it. She excused herself and went upstairs. She was exhausted. She dropped to her bed and stared at the ceiling. She was bone weary, but images of Josephine's face and family kept her awake. A deepening gloom was settling over her. Weeping for her own father and Josephine's fate, she pondered her own unknown but certain end.

Midnight came and still she couldn't sleep. Sitting at the room's small desk, Nora looked out at New York. The icy moon seemed to light up the whole world, but not hers. She thought about what Lil had said in the restaurant. She returned to bed and finally drifted off. The night passed.

The following day, she awoke early. When she'd come downstairs, she told Lil, "Images of Josephine and her family haunted me all night, but I'm not going to give up yet."

"That's wonderful, dear! Now come and sit. How would you like your eggs?"

"I don't really feel like eating, Aunt Lil. Maybe I'll just have coffee."

"As you like, my dear."

Nora poured herself some coffee. Clutching her cup, she wandered around the kitchen and then out to the living room. Sitting, she read the morning paper, mussing it up just as Gerry liked. Then she went upstairs and took a shower. She dressed and went to Lil's salon. Throughout that day and into night, Josephine and her family remained vivid in her mind.

****

Roughly a week after Nora worked on Josephine, as she and Lil took afternoon tea in the living room, Lil asked, "Nora, how would you feel about working on a young woman?"

Nora wasn't quite sure what Lil was saying. "You don't mean at the salon, do you Aunt Lil?"

"No."

"Um, I don't know. How did she pass?"

"That's why I… she hanged herself. Would you be comfortable with that?

"No," Nora answered, "of course not. But I'll do it. As long as you're there."

"How would you feel about doing this alone?" her aunt asked.

"Horrible. Terrified."

Aunt Lil was pensive for some seconds. "Would you confront both those emotions if I asked you to?"

"Yes." She could barely believe she'd said it. "I mean, I think so. When?"

"Tomorrow," Aunt Lil said.

"OK," Nora said, setting down her china cup and starting for the stairs. "I need to go to my room." As she ascended the stairway, thoughts of being alone in that cold, sterile room without Lil to ground her felt… terrifying. She lay down but couldn't sleep. After a restless hour she went downstairs again.

"It will be all right," Lil insisted over dinner. "Once you've done this, you'll understand your fear much better; you'll see how inane those fears were. Please, just relax and focus on the job."

The next day came too fast. As she drove to Unbridled with Lil, she could barely keep down the small bowl of oatmeal she'd consumed. When they entered Neal's office, Lil blurted out, "Neal I think Nora should take the suicide. She has been doing very well alongside me. As her mentor, I recommend her first solo job."

Hunched over his desk, Neal looked slightly taken aback. Raising an eyebrow, he looked at Nora. "Well, Nora, what do you think? Are you ready?"

Nora thought about saying she was too afraid. She would then simply work alongside Lil and deal with the disappointment her aunt would no doubt radiate. But she knew she could do what her role model was asking.

"I…" she looked into Neal's eyes, "I can. I will. Yes."

"Great!" Neal slapped the desk. Lil was beaming with pride. "Then get to it, Missy!"

Nora started for the door. Lil began to turn too, but Neal interrupted her. "Lil, can I have a word with you?" he asked.

Nora, not wanting to be separated from her aunt yet, hesitated. "Just give us a minute, honey," Neal said.

Nora went out but, uncertain what to do, stopped in the hallway.

"Her father committed suicide, right?" Neal asked Lil.

Lil cleared her throat. "I know it seems a little callous, but I really think this will help Nora face some demons. I don't think she ever really got over that… *episode.* Facing a similar suicide might help her cope with her anger and crippling fear."

"Well," Neal muttered, "let's hope this theory of yours doesn't… I don't even know. Backfire?"

Fully aware that she shouldn't have been listening, Nora hurried toward the makeup room. It was the same as she'd last left it: sterile and smelling of formaldehyde. Approaching the table, Nora peered down upon the young woman: Dark bruising ringed around her thin neck. The girl was beautiful. The tag on the table gave her name: Andrea Barlow. She'd been 32-years-old.

She remembered her father swaying beneath the oak, his eyes closed, his body eerily limp. She remembered the dark ring around his neck as the firemen removed his impromptu noose. She stood as still as she had when her father was being wheeled past her, toward the coroner's truck. And here was Andrea.

Her heart, thumping against its cage, seemed to want out. She thought she might faint. Her hand gripped the table. Childhood memories rushed in; Christmases, Thanksgivings, birthdays, picnics, parties. The happy times she'd spent with her father were now murky remembrances. She couldn't help feeling responsible for her father's death, as if she hadn't done enough to help him see.

As she looked at Andrea, a single tear fell. The young woman's face was so lifelike still, as if caught in daydream. Her lips were partially open, as if she was whispering some dark secret. Her hands were lying palms-up alongside her beautiful, tall, model-like body.

Nora succumbed to a brief period of shivering before beginning. She began to work on Andrea's neck, covering the dark bruise with foundation. As she worked, she continued recalling her father. After completing Andrea's neck and face, she combed her hair. She then applied red nail polish to each finger, diligently and one at the time.

Nora looked at Andrea. She was content with her work. The young woman was transformed. Her bruises were covered, her face in peace and her skin was no longer pale grey. Feeling life's fragility in that moment, Nora thought that the bodies to be merely vessels for spirits. Suicide, she realized, was a decision made solely by the soul that inhabited the body. Her father's death wasn't her fault; it was his choice. It was a choice that altered her family's lives for the worse. And neither she nor her mother nor her brothers were responsible.

She tidied up the workplace and then left to see Neal.

"That was crazy," Nora blurted out as she rushed into Neal's office. Lil was there, sitting in one of Neal's plush, desk-facing chairs. "I almost passed out at first. Then I cried!" Seeing Neal's warm smile, she absurdly began crying again. "Then I was sure I'd throw up. But I got over it! I learned something really important."

"What was that?" Lil asked.

"I'm not responsible for my father. It seems so obvious now, but I never felt the truth of it until I worked on Andrea. I thought that, at best, that I'd become insensitive, but the the opposite happened!"

A few days later, early Saturday morning, Nora was once again in the makeup room at Neil's funeral home. She'd been called in to handle another case on her own. Quite nervously, she dealt with the desairology for an old woman from Brooklyn. It was rough, but she said nothing to anyone. Later, in the viewing room, a tenor was singing the Carrie Jacobs Bond classic, *The End of a Perfect Day*:


When you come to the end of a perfect day

And you sit alone with your thought,

While the chimes ring out with a carol gay,

For the joy that the day has brought,

Do you think what the end of a perfect day

Can mean to tired heart,

When the sun goes down with a flaming ray,

And the dear hearts have to part?


Well, this is the end of a perfect day,

Near the end of a journey, too,

But it leaves a thought that is big and strong,

With a wish that is kind and true.

For memory has painted this perfect day

With colors that never fade,

And we find at the end of a perfect day,

The soul of a friend we've made.


Being the only music the family had requested, it was repeated several times throughout the service, like a final lullaby for their mother. During her eulogy, one of the woman's daughters said that it was the song their mother sang to her children before bed or when they were hurt or sad.

During the woman's funeral, each of her children wept into their eulogies' notes. More tears fell as the priest read to the mourners. Nora's heart ached for the old woman, and even more for her children and grandchildren.

\*\*\*

The following day, Nora awoke later than usual, feeling emotionally down. When she'd come downstairs, she told Lil, "Do you mind if I don't go to church today? I'm a little tired."

"Of course I don't mind," Lil said. "You've been working hard lately, honey. You deserve some rest. What would you like for breakfast?"

"I don't really feel like eating, Aunt Lil. Thank you, but I'll just have some coffee."

"You haven't been eating lately, honey. I'm frying you one egg. Eat it or don't."

"I will. Thank you."

Nora filled her cup and went to the living room. She read the morning paper. When Lil called her back, she managed to choke down one egg and a piece of toast. When Lil and Gerry left for church, she went upstairs and showered. She was still wandering through her haze when the doorbell rang. Opening the door, she gazed down upon a beautiful floral arrangement. She picked it up. It was addressed to her! Amidst the red and white roses was a card signed by all the old woman's children. "This basket of flowers can't begin to convey all the appreciation we feel for you now. Thank you so much."

Her mood changed instantly. She was tearing up. It was one of the nicest things anyone had ever done for her. And these people were nearly strangers. Their comment was the most wonderful thing anyone could have possibly said to her. When Lil and Gerry returned home, Nora showed them the flowers and said, "I'll never forget the warmth that these brought to my gloomy day."

Lil smiled. "This is what I was telling you about, honey! You'll feel successful when you know you've helped others, even if they don't always respond. This is high praise. You shouldn't take it lightly."

That night, when Nora went to bed, "The End of a Perfect Day" replayed in her mind, melting her heart and evoking an even greater sense of peace.

***

Two days later, Neal called her back in. And then again a week after that. Some feelings of discomfort and sorrow lingered, often coming in waves just as Lil had said, but at the same time, more wonderful gestures came from some of the deceased's loved ones. Throughout her first three weeks of solo desairology, Nora was periodically tormented. Strangely, things were less daunting while working. It wasn't until she walked away from a body that the nausea and anxiety swooped back in. Sometimes images of dead faces would completely claim her.

At home, she would still stare at her bedroom's wall or ceiling for hours. She didn't sleep well. But little by little her nights became better. Her mind's continuous circling diminished. Her aunt and uncle's ongoing counsel were like soothing winds. Over time, even the gentlest breeze will change mountain landscapes. She began to adjust. She advanced toward peace.

As Nora learned to keep clear of obsessing, her anxieties diminished. Just over four months into her solo duties, she no longer saw much point in her initial perturbation. Life was becoming more and more pleasant. She was improving at desairology, making good money, spending fun-filled hours with Rana and Lin and ever picking up more work at Lil's salon, where she loved chatting with customers, hearing their stories. Also, her work on the dead was slowly becoming more relaxed.

Every week, Neal called for her at least once. She was adjusting to greeting the mourning families. Yet her question remained as to why people desired such nice clothing and makeup and expensive caskets for the deceased, let alone burying them with treasured things. She wasn't about to voice such concerns to anyone but Lil and Gerry, but she didn't think she'd ever completely understand funerals. Slowly but surely, Nora was making a name for herself as a young desairologist. She was on a roll and her skills continued to sharpen. She was in good spirits.

Knowing Nora had a strong passion for writing, her uncle continuously encouraged her. In November of 1988, she began writing about her new life, taking notes about the people she met in the salon or at the funeral home, citing their varied reactions to weddings, deaths and births. Increasingly, she understood that everyone was part of life's cycle: a physical link in the endless chain of beginnings and endings. And she felt such understandings pulling her toward mortality's edge. 'Your turn is coming,' said a whisper in her head.

Often, while writing, she could find no words to demonstrate the love or the partings she'd witnessed. She thought that one thing connecting almost everyone during the funerals were the gaping holes in their hearts and the depths of their feelings. She was recognizing that even the most contended people sooner or later experience life's sorrows.

Fever

Christmas was fast approaching. Anticipation built throughout early December. Nora knew her family expected something more than a card from her this year, especially her brothers. She and Lil spent a lot of time in each other's company, working side by side at the busy salon, decorating Lil's home and business and Christmas shopping. They enjoyed walking in the cold evenings, marveling at the bright decorations and the trees displayed in so many windows. Nora had changed a lot. She was feeling increasingly accomplished and interested.

A week before Christmas, Lil became very sick with the flu. Beset with horrible pains and a high fever, she spent most days entirely in bed. Nora and Gerry brought her tea, meals and medicine. Nora covered almost all of Lil's salon appointments, but a few customers just wouldn't stand for it. Nora, feeling energized, worked long hours in the salon, took care of Lil and did almost all the housework and cooking.

On the day before Christmas, Nora arose early. She was in the kitchen preparing breakfast when the telephone rang. Fearing it would awaken Lil, Nora ran to snatch up the phone. "Hello?"

"Hello, Nora? It's Neal."

It was quite surprising. He was supposed to be away, visiting his sister in Connecticut.

"Hello Neal" Nora said. "Merry Christmas! How's Hartford?"

"I'm not there." He sounded quite distressed. "Can I talk to Lil?"

"I'm sorry, Neal, but Lil's really sick. She's sleeping."

"I'm sorry to hear that."

"Is there anything I can do?" Nora asked.

"Listen," he said, "I have an emergency assignment for tomorrow; can you handle it?"

"Tomorrow?" she asked, mildly surprised. "Tomorrow's Christmas, Neal."

"This is very important, Nora. I wouldn't be asking otherwise. I'll consider it a great favor if you'll help me."

"But it's *Christmas*," she repeated. "Couldn't the family wait until after? I mean…"

"No, honey," he said, "death waits for no one. And these circumstances…"

"Can you ask someone else?"

"No, this client is… *special*. We have to keep his identity completely confidential. No one can know he's here."

"Why?"

"I can't give details, Nora. Suffice it to say he's well known. He passed suddenly yesterday. I promised his family complete discretion."

"Is he a celebrity," Nora asked, "or a politician?"

"As I said, I can't…"

"Who is it, Neal?" asked Nora. "Would I know him?"

Ignoring her, Neal explained, "His brother's a childhood friend of mine. He called last night. The family wants a quick and very private service. I couldn't say no to him."

"Who is it, Neal?" Nora pressed, surprised by her insistence.

"I'm sorry but I really can't disclose his name, at least not now. Many people know him. That's the problem. Nora, I can't tell you how important this is."

She sighed. "But this is my first Christmas here in so many years; I want to stay with my family. Besides, Lil's really sick; I have to be here."

"I'll triple your pay."

"It's not about *pay*, Neal! You know I'd help you if I could."

"But you *can*, Nora. You're the only one who can."

She wanted to refuse, but couldn't. Neal had simply been too good to her. "Okay, Neal, I'll do it."

"Thank you," he said, "I can't tell you how much I appreciate this. Can you be here at five?"

"In the morning?" she asked, surprised.

"Yes, the family will arrive at seven o'clock for a quick viewing."

After a short pause and a deep breath, Nora said, "Sure."

"All right, see you tomorrow then. And please, give my best to Lil; tell her I wish her a fast recovery."

"Thank you, Neal. I will."

"And tell me you'll keep this job under your hat. I need to hear it."

"I will. It's under my hat. Goodbye."

After hanging up, she returned to the kitchen and sat at the small, round table. Sipping coffee, she gazed at the butterfly chime outside the window and thought to herself, 'Who could be so important that Neal wouldn't even mention his name?'

Gerry came downstairs to find Nora staring into her coffee.

"Good morning, Uncle Gerry," she said.

"Good morning, honey."

"Is Auntie Lil up?"

"No, she was coughing all night. She's just fallen back asleep."

"Ok, I'll check on her later."

Once Gerry sat down, she told him about her makeup assignment. Her lack of enthusiasm was obvious.

After listening, Gerry asked, "Neal wouldn't say who this guy is?"

"No, it's some huge secret."

"That's odd."

"Well, I'll find out tomorrow. I'll let you know then."

"If you promised secrecy, you'd better not tell anyone, *especially* me."

"Working on Christmas Day, with Aunt Lil so sick… it's just not right."

"It must be a pretty big deal. You want to help him, don't you? After all he's done for you, consider it an opportunity."

"It is," she agreed. "I'll do it, but I want to be here."

"It'll be fine, Nora. I'll take care of Lil. Don't feel guilty. I'm glad you're helping Neal."

They both went to work preparing a meal. After eating and setting aside a tray to for Lil, Gerry said, "I've got to go to the office for a while."

"On Christmas Eve?"

"You bet, honey. Information never rests. I'll be back shortly. Don't wake Lil. We'll tell her about your surprise assignment when I get back."

"Okay."

After washing the dishes, Nora went upstairs to check on Lil. Standing silently by her aunt's bed, she watched her sleeping peacefully. She tiptoed out and returned to the kitchen. When Gerry came back, he and Nora told Lil about the Christmas assignment.

"Well, this is highly unusual," Lil said. "In all my years, Neal's never requested anything like this. I'm so glad you're here to handle it, darling."

Nora spent Christmas Eve taking care of her aunt. As night fell, Lil felt a little better. She kept her usual upbeat spirits and even came downstairs for supper. It was eleven o'clock when Nora went to bed. She said her prayers then snuggled under her comforter. Gloom settled over her. It was difficult to sleep. Although she was exhausted, her mind would not rest.

The next day, long before the sun had risen, tense with anxiety and anticipation, Nora woke to a cold morning. Lethargically, she got dressed and put on her heavy overcoat. So as not to awaken her aunt and uncle, she tiptoed downstairs.

Her feelings were all over the place as she pulled on her boots in the portico. She was still burning with curiosity to know who the dead man was, yet what she really wanted was a nice breakfast with her aunt and uncle, and then to open gifts with them. Aside from her curiosity, she had no desire to go to the funeral home. As she stepped out the front door, she was looking forward to returning home as soon as possible.

It was a cold, dark Christmas morning but the air had a sharp freshness to it. She drove Lil's car. Just before five, she arrived at Unbridled Spirit. This was the earliest she'd ever been there. It was fairly spooky in the parking lot; bare brown trees all around. There was some light from Unbridled's windows. She parked and got out of the car. Thin sheets of ice covered the parking lot. Walking quickly toward the funeral home, a stiff wind blew her toward the front door. As she stepped into the building, a wonderful wave of heat enveloped her.

Neal and Evelyn were conversing in front of the walnut receptionist desk. Evelyn was taking notes. Nora interrupted, "Good morning."

"Good morning," Neal said. "Thanks for getting here on time."

"What's all the excitement about?" Nora asked.

Neal peered anxiously into her eyes and said, "There's no time to talk about it, Nora, you have to get to work right away; the family will be here in less than two hours."

Nora's cheerfulness evaporated. She could see how troubled Neal was.

"OK," she said, "I'll start at once."

"I'll let George know."

He picked up a phone. "George. Nora's here," he said. "Transfer the body."

As Nora rushed down the hallway toward the makeup room, she heard Neal telling Evelyn, "If reporters show up, call the police. We can't prevent them from gathering in the street, but we have to keep them off the property."

Nora realized, even more deeply, that something highly unusual was happening. She was almost eager to work on the mystery man. She entered the makeup room, turned on the lights, and closed the door behind her. The body wasn't there yet. George was probably en-route. As usual, the place smelled medicinal. She put her purse on a small table by the window then removed her coat. After donning a frock, she waited in tense silence.

A few minutes later, George entered backwards, pulling a wheeled table. Nora was at a rolling makeup station, rearranging cosmetics. Looking up, she said, "Good morning, George."

"Good morning, Nora." Pushing the casket to the center of the room, he said, "Here's our big-shot, your chance to make a name for yourself."

"Oh yeah," she said, "what a treat to be here on Christmas."

"Worth the trouble," he said. "This is a pretty big deal."

"Right. I'd still rather be home."

"Sorry to hear Lil's sick," George said, locking the rolling table's wheels with his foot. "How's she doing?"

"A little better."

"Glad to hear that. Tell her I hope she gets well soon."

"I will."

Nodding, he said, "Do you know who this is yet? Any idea…"

"No," she responded. She wanted to ask questions, but figured it was smarter to focus. "I'm not really interested," she lied, giving George a cold glance. "I'm just here to do my job."

"Oh, *really*!" he said in comic surprise. "You thought about it all night, huh?"

"Not really," she lied again. "It's none of my business."

"How can you not be curious?"

"Honestly George, I don't care," Nora said coldly. "And I'm in a hurry. Neal needs this rushed and I want to get back home."

He actually winked at her. "I don't care either. Couldn't give a hoot."

Pointedly, she glanced at her watch; she had much to do. Her patience was wearing thin. Nora stared at George. She found him difficult to bear sometimes. She thought him a clownish man who was overly fond of joking about the dead. Making her uncomfortable seemed to amuse George. He was taking his time, grinning at his own thoughts.

"George, I'm in a hurry. I've got to get home. May I begin?"

George's smile thinned. "Sure. I know when I'm not wanted." He unlatched and opened the casket then shot an odd glance at her. "Guess I'll go now. See you shortly. Call Neal as soon as you're done."

"Yup," Nora replied with an ill-tempered relief.

As soon as George closed the door, Nora gazed into the casket. She didn't think she recognized him but something was familiar. There was a tall, bearded old man with a mass of tangled, curly, gray hair that looked like it hadn't been combed for weeks.

The man had mud-colored skin. His shirt was high-quality and very white. His tie was red and his suit the color of a blue jay. His attire was certainly immaculate.

When she studied his face closely, she was jolted with disbelief. She'd seen him on the news and in press clippings so many times. Her knees went limp and her stomach rolled. It was Dennis Pino. She flushed. Something fell in her heart, in a long, sickening plunge. Stunned, she held her breath. For a long minute she stood there in shock. She gazed fixedly at his frozen eyelids and marble lips, then the stiffening hands, one resting atop the other.

A shiver went up her spine. Disbelief was turning into rage. Her veins heated. Pink with expanding anger, she whispered, "You *bastard*!" She couldn't imagine doing makeup on this son of a bitch. '*This* is my first Christmas back from California!?' she thought. The whole thing was beyond her. She felt like a caged lioness, restless, impatient. Thinking of her father and family, she averted her eyes from the body, wondering what the hell to do. Anger was turning into panic. She couldn't make that bastard *presentable* for God's sake. 'What was Neal thinking?!' her mind raced. 'Hadn't he *known*...' But there was no reason he should've, not unless Lil had told him. And the family's troubles weren't the kind of thing she would've casually mentioned.

The silence was total. Memories of her father's death hit her like a cold blade. A hundred recollections marched through Nora's mind, all of them undisputedly proclaiming her hatred. This man had robbed her father of life and trapped her family in a tunnel of misery. She could still see her mother in Crestline, crying miserably over her father's suicide. To this day, her mother had never recovered. She probably never would. Remembering the hundreds of *little people* who had trusted this man, she felt ill, hot and cold at once. Tears of fury filled her eyes. She sat there, trying to think what to do. Should she just leave or…?

'This is the answer to your prayers!' she thought. 'The prayer you prayed every night. *Fix* him! Show him what you think of him!'

'But *why*?' a gentler voice queried. 'He's dead. Do you really think revenge will help anyone? Remember what Aunt Lil told you: 'Never judge the dead.' Life is about love and forgiveness, isn't it? When a person dies, no matter how villainous or hateful he or she has been, we never speak ill of them. All the dead find great respect in my country, certainly far more than the living.'

But the old hatreds had settled. She was too weak to resist them. The vengeful desire didn't wane. She couldn't tolerate helping this creature. And for whom? His accursed family?

She looked at him again. Pino lay flat on his back, with the makeup light full on his face. A network of tiny lines, finer than a spider web, coursed his eyelids. Studying his hands, she recalled Gerry's words, "Man is born with his hands clenched; he dies with them wide open."

The voices were like screaming crows perched on Nora's head. She shut her eyes tight, and kept them shut. The heat of her anger dried the tears in her eyes. When her hands grasped Pino's, she found they were trembling. His hands were cold and stiff as a doll's.

In her mind's eye, she saw what she would do: She quickly trimmed and filed his fairly long nails. When they were fashioned into sharp talons, she mixed polish colors into a sickening green hue. She painted his entire hands. When the demon claws were finished she moved on to his mask.

She touched his face then drew back her hand. It shook her. She leaned back and ran her hand across her forehead. She'd always despised cruelty. Her aunt's words resumed playing, "Never show any insensitivity to the dead. The dead should receive as much respect, even more, than the living. Remember that. Never let it leave your mind."

For a second she felt sympathy. Could she fix what she'd done to his hands? Should she? But thoughts of how many he'd hurt kept after her. How many were cheated by this high-and-mighty so-and-so? And he *never* apologized, not once. He'd even complained to his family about the inmates he was confined with, saying he was being treated like a *Mafioso*.

She felt that, if there was a God, if there was real justice, then Pino would have been more severely punished. She felt there was no guarantee of any divine justice after death. Now she had this opportunity… Why not? The malicious thoughts kept cawing, 'Don't wait! If you stop, you'll regret it for the rest of your life! *Do something!*'

Then she breathed deeply. 'Stop taking this personally,' she thought. 'Find goodness, kindness, wholeness, humanity'.

He needed a shave. She picked up the battery shaver and leaned forward. With shaking hands, she touched it to his icy face. She started to delicately shear his beard. Her hands were tensed.

Rage refilled her mind. Then she was horrified by her own intent. Sweat dripped over her eyelids. She trembled in silence.

Finishing, she looked at him. Time dragged. She'd never felt so conflicted before. It was scaring her. Her mind had become a battleground between two strong forces; forgiveness and revenge. It was such a new, foreign feeling.

She would have liked to leave but something held her there. She couldn't let go. She didn't know how much time went by. She felt completely drained. 'Be calm,' her mind whispered. Without taking her eyes off his freshly shaved face, she thought, 'Justice didn't act. Now I can.'

She wouldn't allow him to leave this world with a peaceful countenance. No, she would do something awesome, something *fitting*. The joy of punishing found its climax in justification. She whispered to herself from a heart full of hate, "Nothing is finer than vengeance. An eye for an eye, a wound for a wound." She checked her watch. Time was passing quickly. She didn't care about her job or what anyone would think, not even Aunt Lil.

She neatly brushed Pino's hair back, then carefully applied the lightest color foundation. Her mind raced ahead of her. She would make up him like a demonic joker with heavy makeup; great gashes of ruby ballooned his mouth and his eyes were blue diamonds with wide streaks of black. His eyebrows became dark green like his hands, highly arched and appalling.

Seeing herself smearing great streaks of garish color, her aunt's voice rang out: "Key questions you must ask yourself are: What am I doing for others? How am I thinking of them? Are my thoughts and acts prompted by love, as I would have them think of me, or are they born from dislike, revenge, bigotry and condemnation? And remember Nora, the forgiver tastes its sweetness; only those who dwell in peace can know its measure."

She thought about Neal and his kindness toward her. Finally, her anger settling, she worked quickly but calmly. When she finished, she leaned back and studied her work. Satisfied, she felt she had to get out of there immediately. She couldn't just leave without seeing Neal. Could she? It was twenty to seven when Nora stood. She was so excited to get back home and tell her aunt and uncle what she had done to her enemy. She went to the phone and called Neal. "I'm through," she said, "he's ready."

"Excellent," Neal said. "Thank you, Nora. Thank you so much."

She cleared her throat. "Can I leave now?"

"Oh sure," he said. "Go home. Enjoy your Christmas. I'll send George in shortly."

"Thank you so much," Nora replied, knowing her aunt and uncle would be tremendously shocked to hear she'd worked on Pino and to learn of all she'd done to him.

"Enjoy your holiday," Neal said. "Rest well and give my best to Lil and Gerry."

"Thanks," Nora said. "I will. Goodbye."

She hung up. She was so happy that she wondered if anything else really mattered. She changed into her coat then picked up her purse. Excited, she dropped it. She snatched it up again and then walked back to the casket. "Mr. Pino," she said, bending low over his corpse, "have a *Merry* Christmas."

Then she rushed from the room. She walked hurriedly down the hall, past the empty front desk. Opening the front door, she felt much lighter as she stepped out into the biting air. A frigid gust of wind buffeted her. Under overcast skies, she paused. Coolness settled over her, stillness long wanted. And somewhere in the back of her mind a voice said softly, 'You can move on…'

Three cars were entering the drive, led by a black Cadillac with gold rims. A handsome young man of around thirty years was behind the wheel. She stood watching as they parked. Two middle-aged women in black dresses and an old man in dark suit were getting out of the Cadillac. They slammed the car doors. All looked very solemn, with true misery in their eyes. As she stared at them, fury refilled her. She was, once again, delighted with her work.

She rushed down the steps and, still staring at Pino's loved ones, hurried past them. She was more nervous in that minute than ever before in her life. Looking at the mourners, she was convinced that it would be a long time before they'd feel any happiness. Walking across the parking lot, inhaling the cold, clean air, she thought of all she'd accomplished that morning and how she'd brag to her family. She felt proud.

She slid into her aunt's car then drove. The whole world seemed suddenly marvelous. She felt that her Christmas morning had produced something amazing: her refusal to act upon any thought that wasn't pure, compassionate, and gentle. She felt now free to enter the beautiful, free, and glorious life of abundant love. "I can now have rest and peace at last," she said to herself. With this declaration, the clouds parted, and her mind rejoiced.

As much as she'd wanted to make him reflect the evil clown that he'd been, despite too vivid visualizations, her manifest-self had refused to further demonize him. She had chosen to move on, to leave her haunted memories and anger behind. Storm winds of temptation and floods of hatred had failed to undermine her goodness.

Nora had risen above acting upon resentments and reached a place where hate bowed to right action and compassion. 'For goodness there's only one way,' she thought. 'It is to give up everything opposed to goodness. The old words are right: Love your enemy. God is *love*; love is God. In the end, only *love* matters. But before anyone can put it into practice, they *must strive to understand it*. And this necessitates a self-surrender which few are willing to chance.' Not until goodness filled her in that cold make-up room, could Nora know and possess its blessedness and peace.

## Acknowledgments

My thanks to Phillip Villarreal for his help with editing.

Many thanks to my exceptional friend, Susan Lee Walker for her encouragement and inspiration.